"And who does... simple deman...

A bitter tone tinged his... "Women—especially British women. All the ones I've known, except you, maybe. You work like a man, sometimes speak like a man, but always you remain feminine. You puzzle me." He moved closer, and Jeannie swallowed. "May I kiss you?" he asked huskily.

It was poignant that such a caring man was married to a woman he didn't love. But he *was* married. She mustn't forget she'd been told that. Purposely, she made her voice sound harsh. "You're in no position to kiss me."

"On the contrary, I'm in the perfect position."

As if to verify his words, a cool breeze sprang up, wafting the scent of frankincense toward them. Jeannie's mouth opened in protest and was immediately covered by his demanding lips.

Sara Wood lives in a rambling sixteenth-century home in the medieval town of Lewes amid the Sussex hills. Her sons have claimed the cellar for bikes, making ferret cages, taxidermy and winemaking, while Sara has virtually taken over the study with her reference books, word processor and what have you. Her amiable, tolerant husband, she says, squeezes in wherever he finds room. After having tried many careers—secretary, guest house proprietor, playgroup owner and primary teacher—she now finds writing romance novels gives her enormous pleasure.

Perfumes of Arabia

Sara Wood

Harlequin Books

TORONTO • NEW YORK • LONDON
AMSTERDAM • PARIS • SYDNEY • HAMBURG
STOCKHOLM • ATHENS • TOKYO • MILAN

Original hardcover edition published in 1986
by Mills & Boon Limited

ISBN 0-373-02814-8

Harlequin Romance first edition January 1987

CHAPTER ONE

CLOUDS of dust obscured the view from the plane's small window. As it had circled for landing, Jeannie had seen all she wanted to see; an intimidating, extensive sweep of dun-coloured desert. The contrast with England, seven hours away, was too sudden for her to cope with. Had she made a mistake in taking this job? Far below, a brief glimpse of a primitive air strip and a solitary airport building had added to her uncertainty. Surely she wasn't joining some bumbling, mediocre outfit!

'Scruffy, isn't it?' murmured the man next to her. 'Don't worry. Safiq city isn't like this.'

Jeannie nodded absently. She had been trying to avoid the man's overtures ever since they left Heathrow. Women travelling alone seemed to be fair game for temporarily unattached men.

She busied herself adjusting her watch to Safiq time. Somehow she had lost four hours of her life!

'Ladies and gentlemen,' announced the stewardess, 'please keep your seats until we have come to a halt. We regret the diversion to Kur airport and hope you have not been inconvenienced. For those of you who have no transport, there is an airline coach waiting to take you to Safiq. British Air hope you enjoyed the flight and that you have a pleasant stay in Riyam.'

Smiling wryly at the stylised method of delivery, Jeannie waited for the majority of the passengers to disembark before she reached up for her bulky shoulder bag. The longer she stayed in the plane, the cooler she would remain. And for some reason, she was suddenly reluctant to face the challenges ahead.

But the plane was soon empty; she could not put off the moment any longer. When she stepped out, the heat enveloped her like a suffocating blanket, dust rising in the hot wind to settle on her white shirt. Damn! It was already rather crumpled from the long flight. Now she would look even more of a mess.

And how they had the nerve to call this an airport ...! It was irritating enough that they had not landed at Safiq, without being subjected to these inadequate facilities as well. The grey efficiency of Heathrow seemed almost preferable in contrast.

With an inward sigh of resignation, Jeannie handed her passport to a white-robed Riyami.

'Welcome to my country, Mees Bennett.'

She lifted one eyebrow disparagingly, and he grinned.

'There is a leetle wait. You will have your luggage in one, maybe two hours. We have a café,' he added, seeing her quick frown. 'You will like the chicken.'

'Exactly what *is* the delay? Why can't I have my luggage?' she asked tightly. All she wanted was to get to civilisation and a good bath.

'The porters. It is their lunch break.'

'There must be other porters.'

'No, Mees Bennett. This is only a leetle airport. It is good chicken.'

With an apologetic shrug, he turned to the passengers behind her and she was left to fume at the delay. There was nothing she could do about it of course—and she was hungry.

'Lady ...'

'What do you want?' she said sharply to the plump little boy who was barring her way.

'He will carry your bag,' murmured the passport officer diffidently.

'No, he won't. I can manage.'

To her astonishment, both the officer and the boy stepped forward and gently removed the heavy bag from her shoulder.

'You will not pay. It is a service,' said the Riyami softly. 'Ladies cannot carry these things.' He gave a nod to the boy, who wandered towards the café on her right.

'If that little scrap can manage it, I can,' replied Jeannie, but it was too late. The little scrap had claimed a table and stood waiting for her.

The café certainly looked inviting. A candied green and white-striped awning had been hung beneath the crude steel girders of the roof, and an ambling gardener was watering the huge tubs of parlour palms which bent their fronds over the diners, giving the illusion of an oasis.

'*Fi man allah*,' said the child, laying down her bag. 'May you be in God's keeping,' Jeannie translated, smiling in her embarrassment that briskness should bring such a courteous response. By the time she had brought out a few coins to offer the boy, though, he had disappeared. What an extraordinary people!

The chicken dish took a long time to arrive. There was no point in trying to hurry these people, it seemed. Over the protracted lunch, Jeannie allowed the gentle, stately pace of Riyam to wash over her. During the flight she had been building up her expectations and steeling her nerves for the first wave of introductions. At least this delay gave her time to adjust.

Around her, the soft voices soothed her tired mind. Warm perfumes and hot spices slid exotically into her senses. Lazily, she watched the unhurried dining rituals performed by barefoot waiters as they quietly served the steaming dishes. Maybe she had done the right thing in taking the job. Maybe Riyam would suit her, after all.

The low murmurs of conversation continued. She leaned back in her chair, drinking spiced coffee, watching them. It was years since she'd had any leisure like this; years since she'd had time to sit and stare. A mellow peace settled within her. Everyone moved in such a languid way, their faces and bodies seeming so calm. Even the Europeans had slowed down their usually brusque gestures.

It was strange, but even though the Arabs gazed openly at her from lustrous brown eyes, there were no sexual overtones, only a liquid warmth and interest that created a warm glow inside.

So total was the change of rhythm and atmosphere around her that some of her customary sharpness had been smoothed away by the ambience of the cock-eyed little terminal. A hedonistic pleasure seeped through her mind and body. Riyam was working its timeless magic.

Almost reluctantly she noticed her distinctive two-tone grey cases being stacked by the exit door. Slowly, she rose and this time allowed another boy to carry her bag while she strolled the short distance to the door. A slender Riyami stood to one side of it, holding a large sheet of paper which bore her name.

'Mees Bennett, Safiq?' he asked hopefully.

'That's right. Are you my driver?'

'*Salam 'alekum.*' He tapped his thin chest proudly a few times. 'Me Sharfa. You come plees.'

Not long now, and she'd be in Safiq. Oh, for that bath! The blast of heat on her face outside the terminal building felt like a furnace, and Jeannie quickened her pace to keep up with Sharfa's hurrying feet. Ye gods, a jeep! It looked as though it had recently been dug out of the earth.

While Sharfa loaded her cases into the back, she gingerly opened the dusty passenger door.

'No, mees!' Clicking his tongue in disapproval, the driver politely removed her hand from the door and settled her into the seat with great ceremony.

'I learnt to open doors for myself when I was three,' she muttered drily as he revved up and careered down a dirt track. Nothing gentle about his driving!

'Plees?'

'Nothing.' Damn it, he was supposed to speak English.

'You, me, Fallah,' said Sharfa, riffling in the glove compartment and showing her a map. Fallah appeared to be a small village on the way to Safiq.

'Me in Fallah, ah . . .' Sharfa's English ran out. But his graphic mime explained that he had a wife and child in the village. In his excitement, he turned the steering wheel violently, scattering skinny chickens on the track.

'I suppose that's how the café gets its meat!' she murmured.

With an answering, if uncomprehending, grin, Sharfa sat bolt upright in his seat so that he could see better. He really was very small. Ridiculous that he should cosset her—his air of masculinity contrasted oddly with his fragile frame.

'You, er . . . me, Safiq?' asked Jeannie, as clearly as possible.

'No. Said al Saif in Fallah. He, you, Safiq.'

So, the Education Minister himself was taking her on the second leg of her journey! Jeannie looked down at her rumpled shirt and faded skirt with a sense of frustration. Why on earth hadn't someone warned her? She had so wanted to make a good impression at their first meeting. The job was an exacting one and she needed to feel confident that she looked her best. A low-cut open-necked shirt and shabby cotton skirt were hardly suitable attire for meeting your future employer, and convincing him of your competence. Darn, darn, darn!

She'd get Sharfa to stop just before they reached Fallah so that she could change into one of her proper working dresses, and she could pull her hair back as usual. First, she'd sleep. Conversation was obviously out as far as Sharfa was concerned.

The monotonous thrum of the engine dulled her mind, lulling her into a sleep patterned with dreams: wistful, childhood resurrections of her father's warmth and tenderness; his affectionate teasing as he tweaked her long blonde plaits and threw her into the air with a rush that left her breathless and squirming back in the safety of his arms again.

Then her dream switched. They were in the garden, kneeling together in deep concentration, planting out spring bulbs that week before he died.

Jeannie was wrenched violently from the vivid depths of memory. It took a moment of confusion before she realised that the jeep was tilted at a steep angle and that she was wedged tightly against the windscreen.

Sharfa's worried flow of soft Arabic penetrated her consciousness.

'I'm all right. Don't fuss. All right. Good. See?' What on earth could she say to him? She tried a smile and Sharfa relaxed immediately.

Turning cautiously, Jeannie saw a vast boulder plain stretching back as far as the eye could see. They must have driven over that rocky terrain, and she hadn't felt any jolting at all! She was more exhausted than she'd imagined.

From the gentle rocking motion, it felt as though they were perched precariously between two of the smooth boulders. Sharfa must have misjudged their stability. Gradually the spinning wheels whirred to a stop. There was a silence.

'Allah!' breathed Sharfa. He shifted his weight slightly and the jeep teetered for a moment, then fell with a crash on to its front wheels.

While he wrestled with the stalled engine, Jeannie uncurled her legs and pushed back her soft fair hair, catching a glimpse of herself in the mirror on the sun visor. What did she look like? Sleepy green eyes stared back from a sun-flushed face which glowed with an unaccustomed warmth. And her hair! It had dropped in heavy curls around her neck, framing her small face in a disordered cloud. She'd have to tidy herself up. Frowning, she tried in vain to restore some order to her appearance.

It was a few moments before she noticed that the driver had abandoned his attempts to start the jeep and was watching her admiringly. She shifted uncomfortably under his gaze, a faint blush adding to the colour of her face. How stupid to be so unsettled; it must be the heat. If only she could undo a few buttons on her shirt, or pull it out of her skirt to hang loose; that would cool her down. Most men she'd come across would have misconstrued such an action. Here, they'd be disappointed by such unladylike behaviour. She sighed.

'The engine, Sharfa, try the engine,' she said, pretending to turn an ignition key.

He said something unintelligible then coaxed the engine into life, revving furiously and lurching over the last few scattered boulders before entering a deep valley of compacted sand.

If anything, it was even hotter here. A sullen, dry

wind blew, scurrying trails of sand from the looming
dunes which rose hundreds of feet to either side into a
sapphire blue sky. Starkly beautiful, thought Jeannie.
But how much more of it?

'Fallah?' she murmured.

'He comes,' replied Sharfa.

'You said that hours ago.'

'Plees?'

'Never mind.'

He smiled in reassurance, and more time passed. The
languorous heat and the strange sensuality of Riyam
wrapped closely around her. It seemed a lifetime ago,
another age, another world, since she had left Heathrow.

Riyam, reluctantly sliding out of the Dark Ages, was
evoking new responses in her. There was a new
lethargy in her, almost contentment. The journey had
taken so long that time was becoming meaningless.
What would Paul think of her now! A computerised
automaton, he'd called her.

He'd never understood that she couldn't halt her
single-minded ambition. Like most men, he disliked
her aggressive drive. Paul thought she ought to be
settling placidly with a husband and children. Yet
neither he nor any other of her dates had ever
interested her sufficiently; none of them had matched
up to her father.

It had been a mistake to invite Paul back to her flat
that night. She was so naïve, despite her air of
efficiency. It never occurred to her that his professed
interest in music had any hidden undertones.

'You're quite gorgeous when you forget to be prim,'
he'd said the minute they sat down.

Brush-off time, she'd thought, fending him off and
pulling her hair back into a neat knot.

'Let it loose. It makes you look fluffy instead of
icy.'

'Fluffy! I have no wish to look fluffy. Are you interested in hearing records or not?'

'I'm more interested in hearing you whisper in my ear.'

Paul moved back and slid his hand caressingly up her bare arm.

Jeannie felt that she was being invaded. A tight feeling rose in her chest. 'Don't,' she said sharply.

'Come on,' he coaxed. 'We've been out four times and I haven't even kissed you. How about it?'

She rose, pushing her hands through her hair in concern as he followed. 'I must tell you, Paul, I don't like being kissed.'

'Everyone in the staff room thinks you need . . .' He broke off, embarrassed.

'I know what they think,' said Jeannie quietly. 'Just because I keep to myself. When I'm at school, I teach. I'm a darned good teacher. No one can have any complaints about that.'

'But you ought to mix more. Your feelings must be almost atrophied by now. It's almost two months since your mother died and you've not let yourself go once, not even to cry. If you keep your feelings inside you, they can do strange things.'

'I did cry. On the day of my mother's funeral,' she said coldly, hating the memory of feeling so completely alone. 'If I wanted analysis, I'd ask for it. And stop pawing me, I don't like being mauled! If you only knew how incongruous I find your heavy breathing.'

Paul removed his hand from her waist. 'You're supposed to get aroused.'

'Well if I'm not, it's your fault.'

'Nobody's complained before,' said Paul bitterly. 'I don't think you've got the capacity for love. Your mother was a pretty unemotional woman, by all accounts. Everyone told me you were the same but I never believed it. I kidded myself that there weren't frigid women, only poor lovers. Well, I was wrong in your case. But there's one thing I am sure of: it'll take one hell of a man to rock you out of your complacency. I'm not prepared to batter down your barriers.'

What a nerve he'd had! Just because she was able to control herself, and at the moment was more interested in concentrating on her career.

The day after Paul had been so rude, she'd found the advertisement for the job in Riyam. She'd show him what she could achieve! Brimming with confidence, eyes glistening with enthusiasm, she easily landed the post—a plum job co-ordinating primary education in the Sultanate. And all because of Paul! One day, she promised herself, she must write and let him know how she was getting on. A slow smile spread over her face.

'Fallah!' yelled Sharfa in her ear, effectively bringing her back to the present.

'Oh, it's beautiful!' she breathed.

The fierceness of the sun had abated suddenly and the sky altered colour before her eyes. Now a light blue, now scattered with pink clouds, it soared up from the horizon forming a vast roof above the village ahead.

'Please stop,' Jeannie cried.

Reaching into the bag behind her seat, she pulled out her camera. The jeep drew to a halt, raising a small dust cloud whose particles glistened in the rosy light. The sun set towards Mecca. The sky flared red, orange, then the colour of blood, flushing the dunes with a deep russet glow. Behind her, the great boulder plain stretched empty and awesome.

She finished the roll of film and inserted another to take a shot of the palm trees silhouetted sharply black in the fiery sky. Fallah sat silent, high on the dunes watching her. The light died completely. In a flash, the thick velvet night enveloped her and she became aware of a heady perfume blowing from the village, a perfume as strong and sweet as Arab coffee.

'Frankincense,' smiled the driver, as her nose twitched.

Jeannie was about to launch into a mime requesting that Sharfa turned his back while she changed when the perfect peace and stillness was shattered by a series of desperate screams from the village. She whirled to face Fallah, stunned by the sound.

Blazing torches flared in the village. Their flames joined, creating a drifting cloud of pink smoke that spiralled into the starred sky.

'In! You, me, go!' cried Sharfa, pulling her down into her seat.

He drove like a madman towards Fallah, straight through the unattended gate in the high mud wall and towards the village centre. Jeannie could hear men shouting, then a hollow rifle shot echoed around the crowded buildings.

She grasped Sharfa's arm. 'Wait! Don't go there. It could be dangerous. Let's keep out.'

'Mees?'

'Oh, darn you! Sharfa, find the Minister. The Minister!'

They hurtled on down narrow alleyways. Sharfa didn't understand. Jeannie pulled out a letter from her pocket and re-read the name.

'Said al Saif,' she said firmly.

'Yes, mees. Saif,' cried Sharfa. He swung wildly around a corner towards the noise and shot out into a central compound which was filled with a throng of people, before leaping out of the jeep.

Jeannie waited, biting her lip. The extent of the

differences between East and West was dawning on her. Anything might happen. She locked her door as a precaution, and wound up the open window.

Sharfa had finished chattering to a man in the crowd and appeared at her side of the jeep.

'Come,' he said, trying to open the door.

'You must be joking! No, I'm not getting out.'

'Saif. Come. Is right,' insisted Sharfa.

She stared at him and he nodded encouragingly. Presumably he knew where the Minister was. In any case, she'd have to trust him; she hardly had any alternative.

The crowd parted amiably enough to let them through, then closed up behind them, their voices dropping to a simmering hum of expectation.

The scene in the village square made Jeannie catch her breath. On the dirt floor, watched intently by the villagers, were two men, wrestling like demons. Both were so utterly consumed with anger that they seemed unaware of their audience. Jeannie could hear their grunts, and the sound of fists connecting with yielding flesh and jarring against muscle and bone.

A primitive thrill ran through her before she was able to check it distastefully. They must be animals to fight like that.

She could not see their faces. The one with his back to her was tall and powerfully built. The other was much older and definitely weaker. Dirt from the red earth streaked their torn robes.

For a while, the older man held the advantage. It was as if his more powerful opponent was deliberately restraining the fury which was evident in the strung tightness of his muscles. As they tumbled for a moment close to Jeannie, she stepped back involuntarily and caught her foot on the butt of a rifle.

Sharfa steadied her.

'Tarik!' He pointed to the more powerful Arab, who began at last to exert his strength. The muscles in his back stretched the thin ripped linen and he forced his opponent to his knees.

'So who the devil is Tarik?' muttered Jeannie. Sharfa merely gave a smug smile.

Tarik easily gained mastery of his opponent. He turned, and his unnerving appearance made Jeannie gasp with shock. Never, in her admittedly limited experience, had she seen such a face or such a man; blazing black eyes, thick tousled curls, hard carved cheekbones and teeth clenched in fury. In relentless rage he towered over the helpless man sprawled over the ground. But it was the sheer vibrant life in him that held Jeannie's fascinated gaze. She and the crowd were held mesmerised by the supercharged potency that emanated from his body.

He had no need now to restrain the older man; the burning command in his eyes was sufficient authority to hold him to his will. Tarik grated out an order. The man crawled away rapidly and with his disappearance, the crowd let out a soft sigh of relief and drifted, subdued, into the darkened shadows of the alleys.

Only a young girl was left in the compound. In the darkness, Jeannie could just see her, huddled on the ground, sobbing miserably, her long black hair spread in the dust.

Tarik ignored her and strode over to the rifle near Jeannie. As he straightened, so close to her, he caught sight of her European clothes and his curious glance travelled slowly up her slim legs and curving body before examining her face. For a moment, the menacing brows lifted, softening his face, as he took in the heavy coils of curling hair complementing the golden tan of Jeannie's face, and the glistening moss-green eyes, wide and startled. Then his chest rose with an intake of breath.

So near was he, that Jeannie could feel the warmth of his body and see the beads of sweat on his temples. There was no sound but his soft panting. For some reason, she was holding her breath.

He loomed over her, threatening in his power, grasping the silver handle of his ceremonial knife. Was he going to attack her? Was this a typical Riyami? All Jeannie's confidence evaporated. This was a man who would stop at nothing to get whatever he wanted, a brigand, maybe? Tarik exuded male strength and supremacy in the arrogance of his bearing, the cruel curve of his lip, the thrusting powerful jawline. Deep hollows in his cheeks gave him an almost hungry look, as though he had suffered pain. There was pain in his eyes, too; an agony mixed with desire and raw hatred.

Jumping from one culture to another, she faced her first problem. It had never occurred to her that she would meet anyone so uncivilised, so threatening. Why was he glaring at her like that? For some reason, her presence had quickened his breathing and hardened his eyes, and Jeannie was completely unnerved by his reaction.

Men like him, she hated. Masterful, dynamic, ruthless, obeying few rules, they bent the world to serve them.

But for heaven's sake, she could surely deal with such a man! She was almost certainly more intelligent than he. It would be like facing a lion: she'd have to bluff it out.

She folded her arms firmly in defence, across her breasts, stirring with anger at the presumption of his eyes which swept down her body, his penetrating gaze taking in every inch. His eyes rested on the faint gold swell of her breasts, crowding the low V-neckline of her shirt. He looked momentarily at her face to gauge her response, then curled his glance to the neat dip of her waist and across the voluptuous curve of her hips. Jeannie felt a sharp heat flicker through her body, down to her thighs, halting her intended verbal attack.

Too late, she recovered; he was now questioning Sharfa in a harsh voice. The driver touched his forehead, his lips and his heart in the traditional Arab gesture. All the while, Tarik kept his unwavering eyes on Jeannie. Finally, he interrupted Sharfa and waved him away with an imperious gesture of dismissal.

'I go,' said the driver hastily. '*Fi man allah.*'

'What? Not yet . . .'

'Is right.'

Nodding as if to placate her, Sharfa hurried away. Jeannie's hands hung limply at her sides in disbelief, then, seeing Sharfa retreating into the darkness, she made to follow him. A large hand clamped tightly around her wrist.

'No!' barked Tarik.

She spun round. 'Just what do you mean, "No"? Get your filthy hands off me! Sharfa, come back! Damn you, what do you think you're up to?'

Eyes flashing like green glass chips, she dug her nails under the steel-hard fingers which only squeezed tighter.

'Sharfa returns home. You stay with me.'

His voice astonished her. He spoke in perfect English—almost cultured—with a slight guttural accent. His tone was low and soft, even caressing, yet she still felt threatened. Before, when any men had tried to press themselves on her, she had been able to cope with the situation. With this man, she knew intuitively that she would never get her own way. He displayed all the authority of a man used to obedience all his life. An Arab chauvinist. Stay with him indeed! What was he trying on?

She tipped up her chin to glare at him and met only cold hostility in his eyes. Her heart quailed but she forced herself to say briskly: 'Where is the Education Minister? Tell me at once!'

He ignored her. Barbarian!

'Come on, Jeannie,' she told herself. 'Stay calm. Safiq and civilisation isn't far away. Your fears are irrational. He's only a simple villager.'

'You will let go of my wrist,' she said aloud, 'I'm going after my driver.'

'In the dark?'

'Why not?'

'You are afraid. Maybe of the dark. Or me?' He smiled.

'Neither, you fool,' she lied, the haughtiness in her voice betrayed by a slight tremble.

Tarik's lips curved into a sneer. 'Then why do you shake like a tamarisk in the wind?'

Jeannie fought the rising panic. 'I need Sharfa. He's taking me to Said al Saif. I suggest you watch what you say to me and how you behave. Do you understand? Saif is a very important man. He is my friend.'

An infuriatingly sardonic smile flickered over Tarik's face. 'Indeed.' He paused, obviously trying to combat the effects of some private joke. 'He is indeed fortunate. But you do not need Sharfa—I'm taking you to Safiq.'

'You?' The idea was outrageous. She couldn't sit in a jeep with this man on her own. He was just too ... masculine. Through the torn robes she caught a glimpse of a hard muscular chest, dark in the unlit compound. The male smell of him drummed into her heightened senses and distracted her.

'Me.' His eyes swept arrogantly over her body; slowly, sensually calculating the curves beneath her clothes. Jeannie wished she'd worn a bra. He could see too much under the thin cotton of her shirt. She'd never trust him to drive her around the corner, let alone to Safiq.

'Now look, this is nonsense,' she began.

'Miss Bennett, I assure you that I can think of better things to do, but I have my orders.'

If he knew her name, then he might just possibly be a substitute driver after all. And if he wasn't too keen on the idea, perhaps he wasn't intending to ... She blushed at the direction her thoughts had been taking. He probably looked at all women in that way.

'You must appreciate my caution.' She might be able to outface him if she used English words that he couldn't quite understand. 'The appearance of a substitute without notification has created my indecision.'

He seemed more amused than confounded. Surely he couldn't have understood?

'So regal. So English. Just be glad that someone is taking you. It is a long walk, Miss Bennett.'

'I'm sure it is. But I can't just go off with a——' Jeannie stopped at the warning glare in his eyes and chose her words a little more carefully '——with *any* person who claims to know who I am. You could have wheedled my name out of my driver. You could be lying.'

Tarik stiffened. 'Unlike the English, I don't lie,' he hissed.

Jeannie was taken aback at his vehemence. For some obscure reason, he was consumed with passion. He really needed putting in order.

'Before we leave,' he went on, 'we eat with the Sheikh. Don't look so pleased, he does not speak your language. You see, they are untouched by you British here. Without me, you will get nowhere.'

'You'll take me to Sharfa first,' she said, standing her ground.

'Forget him. Are you coming, or will you stay here on your own till dawn?'

Jeannie wanted to stamp with rage. Feeling helpless was a new and unpleasant experience, yet she must keep control of herself or he'd walk all over her. Clenching her jaw in determination, she glared at Tarik, faltering in confusion when she saw how seriously he studied her. There was that flash of heat through her body again.

Flicking back her tumbling hair, she set her jaw determinedly. 'The Sheikh,' she reminded him coldly.

Tarik looked deep into her eyes. 'You still tremble,' he said softly.

Jeannie gritted her teeth. 'Well, it's not in fear, I can tell you. I'm extremely angry. You're pathologically rude!'

'How very English,' he muttered.

'Hmm,' said Jeannie, looking him up and down and gazing pointedly at his soiled robes. Her voice took on a note of scorn. 'How very Arab.'

His eyes narrowed and their fleeting warmth faded. He turned, striding quickly towards the dark and forbidding alleyways. In deliberately lengthened strides, his long legs flashed over the ground, his white robe fluttering dimly ahead of her. She found it hard to keep up and it was humiliating, running after him along the myriad streets. Yet if she didn't, she'd be lost in total darkness.

'Hurry!' he called. 'They'll be waiting to eat.'

Darn him! She felt like a slave, pattering along in his wake. If only her height didn't put her at such a disadvantage; it was ridiculous trying to obtain a measure of command from the level of his chest.

Light running steps sounded behind them. Tarik heard them a split second before she did and whirled around, stopping so suddenly that she cannoned into him. Automatically, he reached out and held her safely, wrapping her in his arms, cradling her for an instant against his strong, warm body. Her senses swirled wildly at the shock of such startlingly intimate contact: his vigour, the subtle male smell of his clothes, the press of her own soft breasts against his chest. His breathing quickened and it was as if a spark of electricity had fired both their bodies.

One of her shirt buttons had caught in the hairs of his chest, and Jeannie gasped. His mouth twisted in amusement as he reached down, his fingers slowly unwinding the hair, his forearm resting familiarly against one breast which rose traitorously in response to his touch. Jeannie's face lifted to his, answering the fever in his eyes for a brief moment before she pulled away, totally confused and ashamed.

A physical distance separated them. Yet they were still vibrantly close. A stranger might have reached out and tried to touch that vibrant power which surged between them.

'By God!' he muttered.

She had no idea what had happened to her. The slow sultriness which had assaulted her senses earlier now served to tune her body to a high level of sensitivity. Forcing back into her consciousness her old abhorrence of such sensuality, she took a deep breath, ready to protest at his familiarity.

But he had turned away, and once again he was ignoring her and she was prevented from speaking her mind.

'Tarik!' The girl from the compound stood close by, pleading with him. She flung herself at his feet and clung tightly to his legs, while he tried impatiently to dislodge her. Reaching down, he began to prise open her fingers, one by one. The girl moaned.

'Can't you see you're hurting her?' All Jeannie's fear left her when she saw the tears in the pretty girl's eyes, and she crouched down protectively. The next thing she knew was that Tarik's hard hands were dragging her upright again.

'Don't you bully me as well!' she gasped furiously.

'Keep out of this,' he growled. 'You don't know what's happening.' The close heat from his body was almost suffocating.

Jeannie recognised the adoration in the girl's eyes. 'I think I do know—and you're bruising my shoulder, you'd better let me go.'

As if relinquishing something unpleasant, Tarik snatched away his hand. 'I'm winning,' thought Jeannie. 'I can control him.'

'Now, listen to me,' she continued. 'I'm not going any further until you tell me exactly who you are. And I'm afraid your behaviour has meant that your superiors will have to be informed.'

He gave a short, mirthless laugh. 'How pompous you sound.'

Jeannie's eyes flashed. 'Pompous or not, you'll answer me.'

'Such authority, Miss Bennett,' he mocked in a sarcastic pretence of servility and awe. 'They call me Tarik. I work in the Education Department.'

Oh no! She would surely not have to work with this man, would she? Jeannie tucked her shirt tightly into her skirt, and continued: 'Doing what?'

He hesitated. 'Ah—seeing to papers, and things.'

'You mean you're a clerk?' He didn't look like one. He didn't act like one, either. More like a brigand.

'Sort of.'

'I would have said you were a beggar in those filthy

clothes,' she scolded. 'You're a disgrace to the Minister.'

Tarik's grin transformed his face, making his eyes laugh and his curls dance as he shook his head in amusement.

'I agree, but it's not easy to keep clean during a fight,' he pointed out.

'You had no business fighting in the first place. I suppose it was because of this girl,' said Jeannie tartly.

'Yes, she . . . ,'

'I thought so. Barbaric.' She was gaining confidence now she knew that this man was merely a junior pen-pusher and, at the moment, very much in the wrong. She helped the girl to her feet. 'Heavens! She's just a child! How old is she?'

Tarik questioned the anxious girl. 'About fourteen,' he said meekly.

His answer struck her momentarily speechless. Well, that was another reason to inform the Minister of the way this man had behaved. What an appalling character he was. Jeannie knew that Arab girls matured quickly, but for a grown man to fight over a child was taking things too far. Her mouth tightened in disgust.

'Well, I think you'd better send her home,' she said. He frowned. 'She comes with me.'

'That's what you think! I won't allow it.'

Tarik glared and set off again, the girl trailing demurely behind. Jeannie tossed her head and made an effort to keep up. Nothing would induce her to share the journey to Safiq with a wild, cock-sure man who fought like a dog for the favours of a fourteen-year-old girl!

CHAPTER TWO

At the far end of the path loomed the Sheikh's large house, lit by guttering torches mounted on wall brackets. Tarik pushed open the carved sandalwood door, ducking his head under the lintel.

When Jeannie stepped into the large open hallway, she blinked at the sudden bright light and the impact of colour. The first impression was one of gaudiness; of bright red hangings on the stone walls, of a thick red carpet on the floor, and many men in silk robes crowding around Tarik. He finally pushed away their friendly arms and knelt before a gaunt old man with a frayed beard.

The room fell silent as the Sheikh spoke in a faint voice, wagging his knotted finger sternly. Jeannie was amazed at Tarik's humble attitude. His head was bowed and he kept nodding in agreement. Then the Sheikh reached out shaky arms and kissed Tarik on both cheeks, the suspicion of tears glistening in his pale eyes.

At this, the atmosphere changed. The delighted throng burst into happy chatter and Tarik was gently persuaded to take the place of honour. They seemed to have forgotten Jeannie was there at all; in the general jostling for seats, she had been left in a corner, slightly apart from the men. No other women were there apart from the young girl, who stood discreetly behind Jeannie.

Tarik held everyone's interest. Jeannie watched as he allowed his friends to strip off his dirty outer robe so that he could wash, with everyone's eyes—including

26

hers—admiring the muscles rippling and flexing under his deep golden skin. In the flickering light of blazing firebrands, his body gleamed as if it had been oiled. Even she had to admit that he was a magnificent sight. His powerful arms knotted as he doused his head with water and splattered the glossy black hair into flat curls on his forehead. Giving himself a brisk rub with a linen cloth, he accepted a clean cotton robe.

One of the men nudged Tarik and whispered, nodding and grinning in the direction of the two girls. Jeannie averted her gaze too late. Tarik's dark eyes were on her. He'd seen her looking at him which would no doubt feed his vanity. Darn! It was all starting so badly.

Finally, Tarik was ready. Huge trays of steaming rice topped with spiced meat were laid on the ground. Jeannie copied the way the men scooped up handfuls of the mixture, squeezing the rice into a ball and using it to scoop up the meat and sauces. She had no idea what she was eating but anything would have been tasteless to her at that moment. Her mind spun from tiredness and confusion over her recent reactions.

Probably, she reasoned, the heat had sapped her strength and her resistance was low. She must watch herself and pace her exertions in this climate till she was used to the sun. She passed a hot, sticky hand over her forehead and poured herself a mug of water from one of the clay pitchers nearby. The coolness brought some clarity to her head and body. Whatever happened next, she would be wiser not to travel with Tarik. In the morning she'd find either Sharfa or another driver.

Down at the far end of the room, Tarik was deep in conversation with the Sheikh. Jeannie didn't like being ignored by everyone; she wasn't used to it. And, besides, her legs were going to sleep. Action was needed.

Presently she rose and sat close to Tarik's right shoulder, aware that she had broken some kind of social code by moving near him. She was too concerned about the journey to care. 'I want you to ask the Sheikh to recommend a driver for me,' she said quietly.

Tarik sipped his coffee. 'I told you, that is my job. I will take you. For the whole exhausting, tedious journey.'

That unreasonable aversion to her again! Maybe he wasn't interested; maybe it was her own imagination. Maybe it was only her subconscious that saw a physical threat from him.

'Stubborn man,' she muttered.

'If you like, I could get you back to Kur in an hour or so. In a short while, you could be home in England.'

Raising her head, Jeannie looked suspiciously into Tarik's inscrutable face. 'And why should I want to go home?'

'Because you'll never fit in here.'

'What makes you think that?'

He sighed and swilled the grounds at the bottom of his tiny cup. 'Because your appointment was a mistake. I know you're supposed to help Mr Chatsworth in setting up schools for Riyami children . . .'

'You know a lot for a clerk,' interrupted Jeannie.

'Yes, and you don't know enough. For instance, you don't know that Arab men won't take orders from you. You don't know anything about the tribes and their ancient blood feuds; how to wait patiently; how to conduct business in the Arab way.' He picked a sweetmeat from a brass dish. 'Everywhere you go, there will be opposition.'

'Ridiculous! No one would have appointed me, if

they thought that. I know what your problem is—you wanted the job for yourself!' cried Jeannie.

Despite the shake of his head, she felt sure she was right. He looked the ambitious sort, and he was probably furious that a mere woman had pipped him at the post. 'Then just explain to me why I was appointed, if I'm so wrong for the job,' she said triumphantly.

'There is a small group in Riyam who believes it would be an example to Riyami women; that it would give them the confidence to go on to further education. I don't think the men can cope with that yet. It's too soon. Most Riyamis are against such steps. Look around you! The people here have hardly changed their way of life in a thousand years. They are content!'

'You can't stop progress!' cried Jeannie.

'Progress! You British are determined to fling us into a western way of life. But we must move more slowly, in our way. You're crushing five hundred years of development into a matter of months. My people can't accept such an ill-mannered rush into the twentieth century for the so-called benefits of "civilisation"!' He spat out the last word.

Jeannie was stunned. If he was right—and he seemed so sure of himself, so convincing—all she had been told was useless. Perhaps the Riyamis weren't ready for innovation. And to be in a strange country with no inside knowledge of which strings to pull, opposed by every minor official ... What an invidious position!

He leaned forward. 'Go home, English girl. Go home. Here, there is only failure—and bitter opposition.'

There was no mistaking the threat in his voice. It could be a genuine warning; it could be just his own ambition. Yet the flare of triumph in his eyes as she faltered merely incensed her. Right or wrong, she

wasn't going to give in to him and satisfy his inflated
ego and craving for power.

'I've no intention of going home. I like challenges.
It seems to me that you dislike the idea of a woman
being your superior. You're worried that I'll show you
up. Well, I probably will. I'm more capable than you
think.' Her voice had risen and had a saw-edge to it.

Tarik gripped the handle of his ceremonial dagger
till the knuckles whitened. 'Your tongue is sharper than
a hawk's beak. With that voice, you sound more like . . .'

The old Sheikh called out something which made
the men roar with laughter and released the tension
that had built up in the room. Tarik sat back on his
heels, running his eyes over Jeannie's body, then
drawled a reply to the whole assembly, creating even
greater gusts of laughter.

'Just what was that about?' asked Jeannie, coldly
furious.

Controlling his amusement with an effort, Tarik
leaned confidingly towards her. 'The Sheikh said we
argued as if we'd been married for ten years.'

'That's not funny.'

'It would be if you knew me. My views on marriage
are well known.'

'And what was your so amusing reply?' she asked.

For a moment, he was silent. Jeannie squirmed
under his penetrating gaze.

'I don't think you ought to hear the exact words,' he
murmured softly, 'but I said that if I was your
husband, I would solve the argument by carrying you
to the lemon grove and there I would make it perfectly
clear who was your master.'

Jeannie mustered the last vestiges of her self-
control.

'I see. You live by brute force—you haven't the
intelligence to win any other way!' she snapped. 'A

typically primitive method of dealing with enlightened women! Tell the Sheikh he disappoints me with his part in this. I understood Arabs were courteous and hospitable.'

He frowned. 'We are. You have been honoured with a place in the Sheikh's house. Women don't usually eat with men.'

'Well, his behaviour has hardly been polite. I can't speak your language yet you've all taken advantage of that by making jokes at my expense till I feel uncomfortable. That doesn't seem like respect.'

'But you were as aggressive as a man,' Tarik pointed out. 'So we responded to you in a different way from other women.'

'Anyone would be aggressive to someone as arrogant as you.'

'Arrogant! You equal me in that, at least!' he growled. 'Coming here and expecting to control my people.'

'It's not like that. I'm here to organise things.' Her voice rose to drown his sneer. 'I've tried hard to learn about your customs, and I intend to get a good primary education system going. Your country needs a network of schools, doesn't it? Why are you trying to stop me? Don't you care about the children?'

Tarik swore under his breath. 'Such fire! Such impressive desires to civilise the natives!' he hissed.

'I ought to start by civilising you,' retorted Jeannie defiantly.

He half rose, his chest heaving in fury, only to be restrained by the puzzled men on either side of him. He subsided, muttering, and picked up a sweet lime, tearing savagely at the flesh with his perfect white teeth.

'A carnivore,' thought Jeannie. 'He looks as though he wants to eat me.'

The room was silent again, all eyes on Tarik. He

glanced up from under his long lashes, rinsing his fingers in the lemon-scented bowl before him.

'Very well, Miss Bennett. We will see how you cope with my country. You have a difficult journey ahead. Very difficult.' His voice was low and dangerous. 'And now,' he rose smoothly to his feet, 'we leave for Safiq.'

'But it's night-time!' cried Jeannie. She needed the daylight to find Sharfa.

'Perfect. Don't you know it's the best time to travel? If you don't, your reading must have been superficial. We have to cross the main part of the Hebbat before dawn. It's a desert without wells; therefore it's wiser to negotiate it at night.'

A desperate tiredness flooded through Jeannie. She was too weary to spar with Tarik much longer. For some time she'd been looking forward to a good sleep in a decent bed; now it seemed she wasn't even going to get that. And all her battling had got her nowhere. She was still bound for Safiq with this insolent, insufferable and potentially dangerous man.

Apprehensively, Jeannie followed Tarik to a white Land-Rover. He spoke softly to the Arab girl, who clambered into the canvas-covered back and arranged herself on Jeannie's bags, which had been transferred from Sharfa's jeep.

'Surely she's not coming with us, after all I've said!' cried Jeannie.

'Why not? Maybe her presence will help me to keep my hands off you,' snapped Tarik. 'You Englishwomen think you're so desirable to us.'

It was apparent that he felt nothing of the kind himself. She pushed down her injured pride. He really was infuriating! She didn't relish playing gooseberry while he carried on an illicit relationship with the girl. As soon as she met the Minister, she'd report Tarik's outrageous behaviour. The idea gave her some comfort.

They set off into the darkness, the sounds of farewell fading into the distance. Ahead stretched the huge and intimidating desert. Tarik seemed to be navigating by the stars, for there was no track, no indication of any route. Occasionally he would glance at the sky and veer slightly to the left or right.

Although the night was warm, out here in the open desert the contrast in temperature with the day was marked. Jeannie shivered slightly. Tarik leaned across and wound up the stiff window on her side, his strong-boned face close to her own delicate one, his breath warming her skin. He paused, one arm still stretched across her body, a small pulse quivering at his temple.

'Haven't you anything warmer to wear?' he muttered.

Without deigning to reply, she opened her duffle bag and took out a woollen jacket, struggling in the confined space to slip her arms into the sleeves.

'Here.' His voice was dangerously husky. He stopped the Land-Rover and, despite her protests, reached around her shoulders and slowly inched her arms into the sleeves, so sensuously, so protectively, with such deliberate movements that her mouth became dry and her breathing uneven. He paused, angry black brows meeting over his nose, then trailed his long fingers lightly over her shoulders towards the buttons of her jacket.

'Don't touch me! Leave me alone!' Jeannie clutched at her jacket.

Tarik snapped back into his seat as if he had been stung. Pressing his foot hard down on the accelerator, he sent the vehicle speeding over the sands at a terrifying pace. Jeannie hung on to the sides of her seat. She had to keep awake; she dared not trust him. In fact, she hardly trusted herself. There was something

about this harsh and hostile man which made her
wonder where her rationality had gone. All her senses
fought against the unwelcome feelings that flowed
through her as she sat, her thighs too unnervingly close
to his. She despised him and his kind, so why did he
rouse in her those odd coils of excitement?

For a long time she sat bolt upright, her head
buzzing with unanswered questions. Tarik kept his
eyes on the way ahead, ignoring her. At last, the
unbelievable tiredness stole over her and she could no
longer stem the tide of sleep.

While she drowsed, Tarik watched her slide down
in the seat and snuggle up like a sleeping child. He
eased down the speed, driving more carefully, glancing
frequently at the woman beside him. Jeannie had
unwittingly disturbed him even more than she thought.
He wanted her out of Riyam as fast as possible. And as
she so rightly surmised, he always got whatever he
wanted.

When she woke, stiff and stale-mouthed, they were
still travelling. The dawn was just breaking, and the
watery sun shed pale golden light on the barren desert
ahead. Jeannie stretched, rubbing her cramped limbs,
then was suddenly aware of Tarik's eyes following the
movements of her hands. He seemed to enjoy her
confusion. If only she dared to comb her hair—but
he'd probably think that was some kind of invitation.
His presence restricted even normal actions, she
thought wryly.

Tarik was rubbing his forehead. 'You want some
coffee?' he asked.

'Well, yes. I'd like to stop for a while,' she said.

He continued driving. She thought he looked
exhausted.

'Haven't you slept at all?' she asked.

'No.'

'Can we stop soon? I . . . I need to—I have to . . .' her voice trailed off in embarrassment.

'See those rocks? I'm making my over way to them.'

She nodded gratefully. At least he had some sense of decency. Last night, she wouldn't have expected such delicacy from him.

The Land-Rover rolled to a halt on a small incline in the hard-baked ground. Ahead stood an outcrop of granite, shattered explosively by the sudden temperature drops at night.

Jeannie clambered out with difficulty, staggering till the muscles in her legs warmed up. When she returned, Tarik was gathering dried camel dung and piling it in a heap inside a circle of stones.

'What's that for?' she asked.

'I forgot the electric kettle,' he said with unnecessary sarcasm. Taking a flint from a slot in his belt, he struck it with the angular *khunjar* dagger that she knew was worn by every Riyami man. Sparks flew from the blade and he directed them on to a small ball of camel hair. He bent low and blew, feeding dung on to the hair until the fire was well alight.

The scene brought back memories. She was crawling out of her tent, a nine-year-old child dressed as a squaw, whooping with delight as she saw her father lighting their camp fire. He'd jumped up, caught her in his arms and executed a silly Red Indian dance around the smouldering heap of bracken. The memory hurt.

'Fetch the coffee pot and coffee and a large bottle of water,' ordered Tarik, concentrating on his fire. 'You'll find them in the back of the Land-Rover.'

She bristled immediately, angry to have him intrude on her personal thoughts. He sighed, misinterpreting her irritation.

'Look, lady, if you're supposed to be my equal, then you should do some of the work,' he growled.

Jeannie turned on her heel and brought everything to him. He ground the green beans in a wooden bowl and filled the pot with water from the plastic bottle, setting it directly on top of the fire.

'Isn't there anything to eat?' she asked. 'I'm starving.'

'Dates, biscuits and dough cakes in the box there. Keep the lid on the butter jar and don't tip it over. And don't eat too much, either. We'll be travelling far and fast before the noonday heat. It's a bumpy ride.'

'I've heard that phrase before,' thought Jeannie. Though with this man, any ride would be a bumpy one! The fresh clean air had given her too great an appetite to heed his words—besides, she'd never been travel sick in all her life. She sat by the fire, munching biscuits and fruit, dipping the soft cakes in melted butter. Tarik ate only a few dates. He threw the powdered coffee into the simmering water, and added some cinnamon from the coffee bowl.

They sat in cold silence till the girl woke and came to join them, pestering Tarik with chatter and provoking a sharp rebuke. She leapt up and ran back to the Land-Rover, crying bitterly. He seemed to take a delight in cruelty to females, thought Jeannie, forgetting his considerable weariness. All she allowed herself to see was his bad temper. They remained by the fire in icy separation, sipping cup after cup of the hot spiced coffee.

Now the sun burnt in a clear and brilliant sky. It seemed hotter here than in Kur and Jeannie stripped off her jacket, rolling up the sleeves of her shirt. She hoped he wouldn't think she was being provocative. Her breasts seemed to be straining at the cotton fabric rather more than she ever remembered. Tarik's

maleness, his all-consuming virility, made her uncomfortably aware of her own body—and his.

Abruptly he stood, kicking dust over the fire. 'We go.'

When he hauled himself into the driver's seat, he
seemed listless, with none of the energy and passion of
the night before.

They drove for hour after hour in the baking sun.
Jeannie began to feel afraid of being inadequate to this
country's challenge. It was so vast, and felt so alien,
that she seriously doubted her abilities. At home,
she'd known exactly where she was. Here, the ground
rules seemed to be different. The hostility she had
encountered from Tarik couldn't be typical, could it?
Surely a mere clerk couldn't understand the real
situation as far as primary education was concerned?
Jeannie stole a look at Tarik. Some clerk! Much too
confident, even though he was tired.

Could she do a good job? She bit her lip. To heck
with him! He'd really managed to rattle her. She felt
drained by the heat, the never-ending journey, and by
Tarik's dominating strength of will.

'Is it always as hot as this?' she asked, lifting her
hair off her neck.

Tarik nodded. 'Overheating, are you?' he murmured
with a low chuckle.

His true meaning was clear; however, she chose to
interpret his words literally. It was too hot but she was
confounded if she would say so! Carefully, she evaded
the question.

'Don't be silly,' she said patronisingly.

He grunted, then passed a tired hand over his
forehead again, pushing back his headdress.

'You look as if you need some sleep,' said Jeannie,
wanting a rest herself from the monotony of the Land-
Rover's motion.

'I do, but we can't stop until we reach the oasis of

Andhur. It's dangerous to stop far from water. We should make it before noon.'

He fell silent again. Their route twisted along deep, dry river beds, and the sun beat in through the windscreen on to Jeannie's body. Tarik wrapped his headdress around his face and pulled it low on his forehead. Jeannie squashed a wide-brimmed cotton sun-hat down on her head but there was no way of preventing the sun from shining directly on to her stomach and she began to feel sick.

Suddenly, she could take no more. She grabbed his arm, not daring to speak, and motioned for him to stop before tumbling out and retching miserably. Tarik got out too, removed her hat and gently slid her sunglasses away. He waited silently, holding her shoulders with the utmost sympathy. Then, when she raised a white and drawn face, he pulled off his headdress and poured water on to it, sponging her face and hands with surprising tenderness.

She felt like a child again, cared for and protected. It was a long time since anyone had been so gentle with her. She shut her eyes tightly but couldn't prevent tears from wetting her lashes. There was something very comforting about Tarik's attentiveness. His hand was caressing her hair as delicately as a soft breeze, tucking the silk strands behind her ears.

'Don't cry, child—child woman,' he muttered. She raised startled green eyes to his melting black ones.

'Allah!' he whispered. 'Breathe deeply. I told you not to eat much. Travelling in the full heat of the sun is bad for the digestion. In any case, you must eat mainly at night when you're in my country. Didn't you read that in your extensive research?'

'No, I wish I had. Oh, I feel awful—can I have a drink of water?' she asked weakly, refusing to fight him till she felt stronger.

'A little. Not too much.'

'Thank you,' she murmured, grateful for an excuse to avert her eyes.

In the glaring light, she had seen how weary he was. He had stepped back now and was massaging the aching muscles in his neck, circling his shoulders to loosen the tension. Deep lines were etched around his mouth and gone was the wild, alert look; his face sagged with tiredness and he seemed suddenly vulnerable.

'How much longer? she asked.

'I don't know.'

'That's ridiculous—you must know!' she cried.

Tarik shrugged. 'Anything can happen, here in the desert. Riyam is a difficult country to live in if you want to work by the clock, Miss Bennett.'

'An hour, two, more?'

'Depends on the track. We may have to make detours if the sand is soft.'

He threw the soiled headdress on to the mess at her feet and scuffed sand over it, till everything was buried.

'Why did you do that? What a waste! It could have been washed!' cried Jeannie.

'It was unclean.' A smile touched his lips. 'You English are so unhygienic.' He turned and slowly climbed into the jeep again.

This time, as they drove, the sun was no longer shining straight into Jeannie's eyes. For a while she was relieved at this. However, there was something wrong; the sun was now behind them, as though they were travelling west.

She glanced over at Tarik suspiciously. 'Just where are you taking me?'

'Safiq.'

'Then I think we're going in the wrong direction,' she said icily.

'Oh? What makes you think that?' he said calmly.

'I'm not a complete idiot! Even I know that Safiq lies north-east and that we're travelling west.'

'You have a compass, then?'

She clicked her tongue irritably. 'Any fool knows where the sun is at this time of day. Unless, of course, the Earth has changed its orbit!'

Tarik flung her a mocking look from under lowered lashes. 'I'm impressed by your practical knowledge. We *are* travelling west. We're taking another route.'

'Why?'

'If I explained, it wouldn't mean anything to you. I have my reasons.'

'That's not good enough. Tell me why. There's miles of empty desert all around us and nothing to stop us going in——'she tried to get her bearings'—*that* direction. Just what are you up to?'

Smiling slightly, he shrugged his shoulders. 'Since I'm driving, and I know my country better than you, my decisions are the only ones which matter. Or would you like to take the wheel? You know the way, do you? Or do your amazing skills stop short of navigation? Fortunately for me, Miss Bennett, you have no choice but to sit there and keep quiet.'

Jeannie frowned. 'I think you're lying. You're not taking me to Safiq at all.'

'Now why would I want to take you anywhere else?' he murmured.

'Because, because . . .' The colour rose in her cheeks.

'Hah!' His scornful laugh startled her. 'Surely you don't think I am abducting you! Really, you do have a high opinion of yourself.' He braked hard and switched off the engine, turning around in his seat to face her.

'If I wanted a woman, then I wouldn't choose you. I like my women to be soft and warm, not cold, hard and aggressive. You will be relieved to hear, Miss Bennett, that even if I felt desperate, your honour—or what there is of it—is perfectly safe with me. I dislike Englishwomen. I dislike their grasping ways, their unfemininity, their desire to dominate and crush any man they meet. In fact, I would rather ravish that child in the back than you.'

Her face flared with humiliation. There was no need for him to be quite so uncomplimentary. 'Then why aren't we going the right way?' she muttered through her teeth.

'We'll turn soon, he said shortly, starting up the Land-Rover again.

They sat in frigid tension for the next hour. The girl behind them began to chatter shyly to Tarik who answered quietly, relaxing his former hostility. Jeannie felt very left out. It was nearly noon and there was no sign of the oasis. She began to fear that Tarik was up to no good.

In the middle of a broad expanse of deep soft sand, he stopped the Land-Rover, supposedly to fill the water tank from one of the large cans strapped on the side. Jeannie waited, the sun pouring down on her, but he seemed in no hurry to move on. The water can was left, unused, on the sand. Tarik's head bent low over the engine as he fiddled with the plugs.

'Is something wrong?' she asked finally, climbing out.

'I think we'll have to wait here while the engine cools down,' he said, looking at her out of the corner of his eye.

'But there's no shade!' she cried. 'We'll boil in this heat! I thought you said we'd reach the oasis by noon.'

'Did I? Well, we haven't. I'm sorry you find my

country so inhospitable. Your delicate English skin is going to get badly burnt, I'm afraid.'

He didn't sound in the least bit sorry. Jeannie flounced off angrily to sit on the other side of the Land-Rover, where its bulk cast a little shade. As she slid to the ground, she flashed a look of hatred at Tarik, to see to her amazement that he was thudding down the bonnet with a delighted smirk on his face. Blast him, he was enjoying her discomfort!

He formed a shelter with his loose cotton robe by sticking a short pole in the ground and draping its voluminous folds over it. like a tent. He pulled the girl into its shade, out of the blazing sun. Jeannie was desperately hungry, being used to regular meals. Infuriated by being excluded—even though she emphatically didn't want to be included—she strode over the sand, burning the soles of her feet through her thin training shoes.

'When do we leave?' she demanded sulkily, feeling very silly talking to two pairs of legs and hunched knees, which was all she could see of them under their shelter.

'Oh, some time,' came Tarik's muffled voice.

Crossly, Jeannie pulled back the cloth to find the girl tucked close to Tarik. A treacherous stab of envy darted through Jeannie's body.

'I'm tired, I'm hungry and I'm very hot,' she said tightly. 'You are responsible for me. Do something about it.'

'There's a few dates in the back. Go to sleep. I can't do anything about the sun.'

'That's not enough for a meal! I want my lunch!' The words seemed childish to her own ears.

With a sigh, Tarik rose and ambled to the stores. He handed a bag of flour to Jeannie.

'What's that for?' she asked.

'Mix it with water, make a dough, push it under the sand and it'll bake,' he said.

'Good grief!' she yelled. 'Is that the sum total of your provisions? Didn't you come prepared for this journey?'

'You ate all the biscuits,' he pointed out reasonably. 'Try pouring some water over your head. That will cool you down.'

'I won't cool down till I get rid of you,' snapped Jeannie. 'And let me make it quite clear that when we leave, I expect us to be travelling in that direction.' She pointed to the north.

'Perhaps in half an hour.'

It was an uneasy rest for Jeannie. To stay in the shade meant leaning up against the wheel and she dozed fitfully, occasionally altering her position to ease her aching neck . . .

'Come on, Miss Bennett, we're ready to leave,' Tarik was slamming down the bonnet.

Feeling woozy from hunger and the shimmering heat, she heaved a sigh of relief and scrambled into the cab, slamming the door. Tarik was checking the back wheels. With a muttered exclamation, Jeannie thrust her head out of the window.

'Now what?' she cried.

'The wheels are stuck. I think you'll have to push.'

'You!' She was speechless with rage.

'Save your strength, Englishwoman. I'll start the engine and you push from the back. The girl can help.'

Jeannie strained and heaved, sweating heavily in the sweltering heat. Tarik shouted encouragement but the Land-Rover didn't budge. Finally, she collapsed on to the sand, exhausted.

'Come on!' yelled Tarik. 'Don't stop! Put some effort into it or we'll be here for days. I haven't enough dates to last that time—not at the rate you eat, anyway.'

Muttering a string of very unladylike curses under her breath, Jeannie put her shoulder against the dusty back once more. With a sudden lurch, the Land-Rover rolled forward, leaving her spread-eagled on the ground, half blinded from the sand which had flown into her eyes.

'What a terrible country this is!' murmured Tarik's deep voice in her ear.

She blinked, trying to clear her eyes, but the hard grains made them water painfully. Large, strong hands grasped her shoulders, hauling her up, and lean fingers tilted her head far back. She opened her mouth to protest, hating to be so much at his mercy and unable to see what he was doing, but shut it in surprise when he cupped her face in his hands, standing so close that she could smell the slight tang of lime on his skin. Despite the heat and their long journey, he smelt fresh and clean whereas she felt unkempt.

'Hmm. I can get some of the sand out. Keep still!' His breath was like a whisper on her skin. 'So much sand! What were you doing to fill your eyes so!'

Jeannie opened her eyes wide in fury and immediately regretted it, peering out of focus at him through blurred curtains of tears.

'Don't cry,' he said patronisingly.

'I'm not crying!' seethed Jeannie. 'My eyes sting, that's all.

'What an awful journey you've had.' Tarik's voice was soothing and falsely sympathetic. As he worked on her eyes, he worked on her strained emotions, too. 'You must be regretting you ever came. The heat, the sand, the unending journeys—you haven't had problems with the flies yet, but you will, of course.' He sighed. 'Not the sort of place for you, I think. Now look, Miss Bennett. We're half an hour from an airport which serves the local oil rig. I have connections with the supplies plane to Bahrain. I could drive you to the airport now and all this could soon be just a bad dream. Something to tell your friends. You won't be letting the Minister down; he'd rather you made your mind up now. He'd understand. Just think: you could be home again. Back home in Sussex.'

'How do you know I come from Sussex?' asked Jeannie suspiciously.

'I read people's files,' said Tarik baldly.

'Then all the more reason I should get to Safiq and tell people about you.'

'It's tempting, though, isn't it? Perhaps we ought to travel in that direction anyway; looks as if one of our notorious sandstorms is brewing.'

For a moment his offer did seem attractive. Her cousin was only using her flat for three months; they could easily share for a while. Jeannie risked opening one eye and looked towards the horizon. It seemed perfectly normal. That convinced her that Tarik was making the sandstorm up.

'I think you're exaggerating. I will *not* be pushed around by you. Get it into your head that you're taking me to Safiq. How much further is it?'

Briefly, there seemed to be a flash of admiration in his gaze, then his face darkened.

'Difficult to say,' he replied.

'You don't give an inch, do you? I hope you realise that your behaviour may cost you your job?' said Jeannie.

Tarik roared with laughter as he slid into the driving seat and revved up.

'I don't think you are that influential!' he grinned.

'We'll see,' she muttered. He'd committed enough errors in one day for anyone to get into trouble. But at least he was going northwards.

'It would be simple to drive you to the airport now,' he persisted.

'Why are you so all-fired keen to send me home?' asked Jeannie.

'It will save you time in the long run. You don't like my country. You don't like my people . . .'

'That's where you're wrong. I love the atmosphere, the pace of your country. It's very soothing. And I like the people. It's *you* I don't like! This journey wouldn't have been so bad with Sharfa.'

'You'll never be accepted.'

'Ben Chatsworth has managed perfectly well, from what I hear,' said Jeannie.

'But he is a man. And he has been here for five years. You are a woman.'

'What have you got against women, Tarik?'

'Nothing, I love to be against women,' he replied crudely. 'Unless they're like you. The idea of working with someone like you fills me with horror.'

'Then you can stop worrying. I doubt that you and I will be involved with each other. Your position sounds far too junior.'

She was being pompous again. She did say some awful things in her attempts to stop him. She leaned her head against the back of the seat. Arguing with him was emotionally exhausting.

To her relief, they arrived at the oasis within the hour. As they approached, Tarik halted the jeep and reached for his rifle. He then drove cautiously into the palm-fringed shade.

'Why are you being so careful?' asked Jeannie.

'There are still bandits in the interior. Or there might be those who need to take retribution against the British.'

'I don't understand.'

'The British sometimes tread heavily with their clumsy feet. My people look out for someone of your race—anyone—to avenge insults, whether real or imagined.'

'But that's unfair!' cried Jeannie. 'Do you mean that
we could be harmed because of the quarrels of strangers?'

'Why not? A man must keep his honour.'

'That's stupid. I . . .'

'Enough!' roared Tarik. 'I don't want to hear your
opinion. We've held such traditions for thousands of
years—before you British formed primitive tribes.'

'That doesn't make it . . .'

'I said *enough*!' yelled Tarik. The sound in the cab
deafened her. 'I am tired. Be silent.'

He slammed out of the cab, carrying his rifle, and
settled down by the pool.

'Wake me if anyone comes. Keep your ears and eyes
open.' He rolled over and made himself comfortable.

Jeannie looked at the girl helplessly and they both
smiled ruefully at each other. She supposed it wasn't
the girl's fault that she wanted to follow Tarik. Arab
females probably liked dominant men. Yet it was with
some jealousy that she watched as the girl curled up
intimately against Tarik's back. Grumpily, he pushed
her away, but when he fell quickly into a deep sleep,
she crawled close to him again.

While they slept, Jeannie spent some time cleaning
herself up, changing her shirt and brushing out her
hair. She rarely wore make-up and there certainly
wasn't much point in this country. Anyway, the
Embassy had suggested she should look as demure as
possible, in deference to Arab beliefs. Her face was
smooth and soft enough and her complexion such an
even pale gold that make-up would have been
superfluous.

As the afternoon wore on, she relaxed, knowing that
Tarik would probably sleep for some time after his
long, hot drive. Out in the desert, the sun was searing
the ground till the fine grains of sand danced in the
heat. When she looked out over the way they had

come, she could see the tiny crystal grains glinting like
minute diamonds. Once again, the raw beauty of the
scenery put her irritations into perspective.

The air filled with the heat, thickening, humming,
the total silence a soothing, slumbering balm. Jeannie
wandered over to the pool. It was surrounded by
thick-leaved date palms which cast dark green
shadows on to the deep blue water. Flocks of swallows
dived and swooped over the pool, dipping in swift
movements to drink from the water. Her slim fingers
dabbled in the cool, clear blue.

The freshness of the oasis brought peace to her
mind. Despite the tiring journey, Jeannie was able to
appreciate the wild beauty of this country. Simplicity
lay in the starkness. Maybe that was what made its
people so dogmatic, so definite in their conception of
right and wrong. Such clear beliefs certainly made life
easier for them, if not for strangers.

Thoughtfully, she eyed the water, then hurried to
find her case. Rummaging through it, she pulled out a
denim button-through skirt and peered around at
Tarik; judging from the heavy slump of his body, he
was still deep asleep. Quickly Jeannie replaced her old
skirt with the fresh one, then pushed her feet back into
her trainers to cross the sand. It was hot beneath her
feet even though they had parked in the shade.

She stooped to take off her shoes and cautiously
dabbled her toes in the water. How wonderfully cool
and silky it felt! Hating the feel of her hot, perspiring
body, she stepped in deeper to her thighs, till she had
to haul up her skirt to her waist. The sand that lay at
the bottom was soft underfoot. She wriggled her toes
and flicked water in the air, abandoning all decorum
and quietly splashing her arms softly backwards and
forwards like a child. A shaft of sunlight broke
through the overhanging palms, its fierce rays muted

by their waving leaves, its mild warmth playing on her upturned face.

For a long moment she stood there, allowing the gentle heat to bathe her body. She undid the buttons of her V-necked shirt and let it fall open, to catch the sun on the swell of her breasts. She felt pagan, a child of nature, a lizard basking in the sun—filled with the illicit feelings which had been so carefully expurgated from her childhood by her anxious mother. How unalike her parents had been! She'd always thought she took after her mother; cool, composed, without emotion. But since she'd arrived in Riyam, she'd seemed more like her father, whose feelings so readily erupted.

Soft fluttering wings whispered in her ear. She opened her eyes slowly. There, resting on her shoulder, was a huge, multi-coloured butterfly.

'It thinks you are a flower,' whispered a low voice behind her.

She turned her head with infinite care, reluctant to disturb the dream-like quality of the moment. Tarik stood on the edge of the pool, clad only in cotton trousers, his massive chest rising and falling like a golden wall. The breath caught in her throat and she felt a stab of heat flash through her body, startling her. He stared at her in a strange, calculating way and she had the impression that he was making up his mind about something.

The air simmered with heat; palm leaves rustled softly. Rippling warm fingers of sunshine caressed her throat and breasts and her lips parted to allow her quickening breath to escape. Keeping his dark eyes fixed on Jeannie, as if mesmerised, Tarik entered the pool barefoot and came to within a few inches of her, waiting with an expectant stillness. He was close enough for her to see that the lashes on his lids were extraordinarily long and silky; the pupils of his eyes

black and unfathomable. She swayed slightly, drunk
with his presence, his maleness, the sleepy warmth
and beauty of the oasis.

'Such a flower,' he murmured. 'Just opening, ready
to burst into blossom.'

Instinctively, she knew what he was about to do. In
this magical make-believe world, thousands of miles
from the realities of home, one part of her was willing
it to happen, for him to catch her up in his arms. The
other was cautioning herself to deny him with all her
power. She had no idea that her struggles showed so
clearly on her face, and in the imperceptible yearning
of her body.

The corners of Tarik's mouth twitched but still he
held her with his eyes and she stepped backwards,
slowly at first, then taking faster steps in the resisting
water until she lost her balance and fell.

Iron-hard arms lifted her up as she spluttered
indignantly. As Tarik drew her closer, she put out her
hands protectively, but before she could prevent it his
bare chest was touching her breasts, so scantily
covered by the shirt. She felt his whole frame shudder
as their cushioned fullness was crushed against him,
and she gasped to feel one arm slide around her waist,
the other touching her hair and stroking its golden
perfumed softness.

'Dear Allah!' he muttered in her ear, reaching down
with his warm mouth to nibble at her lobe. She
struggled ineffectually while a fierce dart of pleasure
shot through her body, she arched her back in
response. Surprised, Tarik stepped back, seeing her
enormous green eyes widen, their depths betraying her
feelings. He groaned and pulled her quickly to him.

'Curse you, English girl!' he muttered. 'I never
thought . . .' He wasted no more time in words.

Greedily, his lips were searching her face, burning

her skin with their heat. She quivered deliciously in anticipation, turning her small face up towards his.

It was as if she was a different woman; no longer Jeannie Bennett, cool, collected and passionless. Now she was living only for the depths of her instinctive responses, barely heeding any normal codes of behaviour. Yet the two opposing forces within her still fought for supremacy.

'No! Stop it!'

Her voice sounded oddly husky and unconvincing. Tarik smiled.

CHAPTER THREE

THERE was a relentless inevitability in the way his fingers gripped her shoulders, holding her so that he was able to press his body slowly against hers. A quick spear of excitement darted within her. She welcomed his touch; she wanted his kisses on her lips; she wanted him to 'win'. The space between their mouths seemed a vast distance that she yearned to close, yet he seemed impervious to her silent call.

She closed her eyes to shut out the sight of his hovering, ruthless lips and at last, at long last, his mouth brushed hers—lightly to begin with, as if relishing the long-drawn-out pleasure, teasing her, playing with her, his mouth felt dry and demanding, hers full and moist. Crushed against him, she could feel the rapid pounding of his heart blending with the rhythm of her own, and the hard strength of his body. Unable—unwilling to escape, she remained locked with him in an unknown space. His mouth wandered expertly over hers, kissing, nibbling, then bruising fiercely while she rocked with passion. His breathing became harsher and his kisses more and more urgent until she felt the hardness of his teeth behind his mouth and the tightening of his arms, as if he was preparing for a struggle. Alarmed, Jeannie moaned into his mouth. He had woken in her a raging fire which set her whole body alight and sent sharp pangs of desire running through her like burning arrows, searing to her loins, travelling new and startling paths.

She could not handle this situation—her own body

was no longer on her side. Suddenly frightened by his intensity, and highly aware of his potent animal lust, she began to fight her reactions in earnest. Attempting to gather herself together, she shifted her hips slightly, ready to push him away and to relieve the burning of her body, but Tarik misunderstood her movement, whispering even more deeply in his own throat, darning her, pressing even harder with his own hips. The intimacy of his body appalled her. She had never been this close to a man before; never felt such urgent desire.

A hawk screamed above. Tarik raised his head and moved away abruptly, staring at her with an extraordinary mixture of raw hatred and longing.

'What kind of woman are you to entice me like that?' he asked softly.

'No,' she began.

'Yes!' he mocked. 'So carefully arranged. A half-naked, green-eyed goddess rising from the pool; charmingly tousled hair, a seductive pose ... How could any man resist such an invitation?'

Jeannie's mouth fell open in astonishment, then clamped shut again in cold fury.

'It was no pose, I can assure you. I was cooling myself down. I thought you were asleep, and you'd better get it into your thick head that I had no intention of attracting you!'

It was true of course—well, to begin with, at least. Jeannie tried to smooth down her wild hair.

'Really? You needn't try to fool yourself, or me. I'm quite used to your countrywomen making a play for me.'

'I've never met anyone so conceited in my whole life,' she retorted. 'Anyway, I thought you said you never touched Englishwomen!'

'That was true until a few moments ago. You have

made me abandon all my principles.' His voice was
tinged with pain.

'You don't know the meaning of truth—and as for
principles . . .!'

'If only you didn't have to open your mouth,' he
whispered.

Again she backed away, alerted by the hard light in
his eyes. In a sudden movement, he trapped her arms
behind her back and kissed her neck wildly while she
wriggled desperately. Then as the tide of pleasure
blotted out her conscience, she became lost in the
sensuous suspense as she waited for the inevitable kiss
on her pouting lips, her breathing now erratic as she
gave herself to the wonderful insidious spirals of
excitement which flowed through her body.

Nothing happened. Tarik was quite still, just
holding her. She opened her eyes. There was a look
of triumph on his face and his arms slackened their
hold.

'As I thought,' he murmured. 'Like all the others,
you can't wait.'

She broke free with a violent wrench. They stood
facing one another, panting heavily, the heat surging
between them.

'You, you . . . Oh!' she whispered. 'How dare you
treat me like that!' Most of her anger was directed at
herself. She *had* been waiting for him to touch her; she
had wanted his kiss. Guilt washed over her. She felt
cheap.

Tarik raised a shaking hand to push back a lock of
hair which had fallen on to his forehead. 'I dared,
English girl,' he said in a tight voice, 'because you
wanted me to. You encouraged me. You accepted my
kisses, demanded them despite your pretence of
horror. You burn as I do—no, don't deny it, I know
very well how much you burn. You might pretend to

be made of ice, Miss Bennett, but even ice must melt eventually. And I think you've reached boiling point; your body is as much on fire as mine.'

'Rubbish.' She must control her wavering voice—it didn't sound very convincing. 'You have a vivid imagination. You don't really think I'd let a man like you touch me?'

'You did,' he said with inescapable logic.

'I mean . . .'

A movement registered in the corner of her eye and made her jump. The girl was watching them stonily. Jeannie gazed with shame at Tarik.

'You succeeded only because I couldn't resist you.'

Tarik smiled. 'Exactly.'

'You arrogant swine! I meant I wasn't strong enough to stop you!'

Neither had she wanted him to stop. There was a terrible unfulfilled emptiness in Jeannie's body. What had this man done to her that was different from any other? He was right; just by touching her, by kissing her with such tender expertise, he had roused her to a pitch she had never reached before. All the subtle dinners, parties, quiet meals and record sessions afterwards—even with Paul—none of these had evoked one-tenth of the confused stirring emotions she was now experiencing.

She was tired, that was it. And hungry. That, and the sun. She wasn't herself.

'You will *not* touch me again, do you hear?' She almost spat out of the words, so great was her humiliation at losing herself so deeply to passion, and at being observed by the young Arab girl.

'But you want me.'

'That's ridiculous! You're imagining it. You've forced yourself on me and used your strength to get what you want.' She tried to convince herself. 'I can't think of anything worse than being assaulted by—by an over-sexed clerk!'

Her words rang into a deathly silence. Tarik's sensuous expression changed to harsh and penetrating hatred with the suddenness of a summer storm. Then his face became impassive, only his jet-coloured eyes betraying the anger within.

'So you've controlled yourself just in time, eh? Before the rough native defiles you with his greasy hands? I forgot. I must return to my place at your feet, bowing low in the dust. I am, of course your servant. But don't pretend to yourself, woman. Admit your passions.' His scornful glance raked her body with satisfaction as a succession of blushes tinted her golden skin. 'Hmm. Still overheated, I see.'

Poor Jeannie felt uncomfortable. She'd given the wrong impression. She hadn't intended . . .

'Take my advice, Miss Bennett. To avoid any unwelcome attentions from men like me, don't wander around Riyam half-naked. We natives are very simple and we get ideas about women like that. I really think you ought to reconsider taking this job after such an exhibition. What would the Minister think?'

He swung around haughtily and splashed forcefully out of the pool, his trousers clinging closely to his powerful legs.

Jeannie hugged her trembling body in an attempt to still its demands. What an idiot she'd been! What on earth had made her act like a . . . She could not bring herself to think the word. And what an awful way to start her new life! She groaned. He'd probably boast about the incident to everyone he met. Maybe even her new boss. This trip had been a disaster. Somehow she must stop him—strike a bargain, anything. Stumbling out of the water, she pulled her skirt down and fumbled with the buttons on her shirt.

'Wait a minute!' she cried.

He'd picked up his robe from the ground and turned in the act of wrapping it around his body. He wouldn't look at her. 'An apology?' he asked in a strangely sad voice. 'Or do you need satisfying.'

Jeannie tried to master her emotions and keep down the anger in her voice. 'You're not to . . . I don't want you to . . .

'Gossip about your shame?'

Why did he always make her feel that she was in the wrong? She'd never thought of herself as racially prejudiced before; he seemed to delight in forcing her into that position.

He stared at her. 'I don't think your colleagues would accept you now. Once they know how you behaved with me.'

'How . . .! Oh, you wouldn't tell!'

'Wouldn't I?'

Jeannie was appalled. He'd twist the whole thing till everyone talked about her and the way she'd let a complete stranger almost make love to her. She thought of Paul. He'd tried to touch her as this man had, but his hands, his mouth, hadn't had the same effect. Her body sprang alive again at the thought of Tarik's assault on her senses.

'Please,' she whispered, spreading her hands helplessly.

He lowered his eyes and turned away abruptly. How could he be so unmoved by her misery?

'Miss Bennett, you must go back to England now, don't you see? You can't stay. What we did will be all round Safiq in the next few hours. If I don't talk, the girl will. Come on, you can catch the six o'clock plane.'

He made for the Land-Rover. Jeannie ran after him, thinking rapidly. She wouldn't let him run her out of

Riyam. Somehow she'd convince the gossips that she was innocent. Naïve, yes, but innocent.

She caught his arm. 'You've forgotten what I know about you. I could probably halt your career if I wanted to. What if anyone heard of your fighting over the girl, and your insolence? I'll keep quiet about that if you don't talk about what just happened.'

He gazed at her from slanting black eyes. 'Don't you ever give up?'

'Not often.' Her chin was up, her gaze level.

There was a long silence before Tarik's shoulders drooped wearily, and he frowned. When he spoke again, he sounded strangely unhappy. 'So sure of yourself. Blindly sure. All right, I can't force you to leave so get in. I'll take you to Safiq. But prepare yourself for an unpleasant shock. And I tell you this, if you're still in your job at the end of your three-month trial period, I'll apologise on my knees. But you won't last a month.'

It had been too quick. She'd expected him to demand money or a promise of help towards his promotion. It was very suspicious. 'Give me your word,' she persisted.

Judging by his furious glare, she had made a mistake again.

'Miss Bennett, you'll have to learn not to demand promises in my country. I said I agreed, and that is enough. I am a Bedouin. If a Bedouin makes an agreement he is bound by it. I thought, Miss Bennett, you had studied my people!'

Angered by her insult, he spun on his heel and wrenched open the cab door, grinding gears in exasperation. Fearful of being left behind, Jeannie and the girl flung themselves into the open back as the wheels spun in the sand and he turned a rapid circle, accelerating wildly into the sunshine.

From the oasis, it was a surprisingly short journey to Safiq. The route quickly became crowded with traders hauling their wares along the overland trails to the capital. Lanky camels plodded slowly and inexorably, weighed down with enormous baskets of frankincense from the mountains, or huge net bags full of dried sardines destined to feed the camels of the Sultan's Desert Corps.

Many of the travellers greeted Tarik as he passed, firing their rifles erratically—and dangerously—or gravely touching their hearts in salute. Tarik returned each greeting with a friendly wave. He was well known, it seemed. Probably notorious: a man who entertained his friends with stories of his conquests. Jeannie wriggled uncomfortably. Could she rely on him to keep his word?

As the track filled with travellers, she was puzzled to see the respect and deference displayed to Tarik as he was automatically given right of way. Obviously a clerk's position was considered a great achievement by these tribesmen.

One of the supplies bags rolled against her aching back. She pushed it away irritably. It was very uncomfortable, perched on the sacks. From the moment they both jumped into the back of the vehicle, the young girl had made her antipathy towards Jeannie very evident, and they had each taken care to avoid body contact, though it was difficult with Tarik's wild driving.

'Come up in front,' he suggested in a low voice after her cry of pain when she banged against the unprotected sides. 'I won't touch you.'

'You're darned right you won't,' she replied stiffly. She was determined not to have anything to do with him, even if it meant getting bruised for her principles.

They crested the Jafar mountains, which curled protectively around Safiq, and Jeannie gasped in delight at the startling view. Below them lay the city, sparkling white in the sunlight, its flat-roofed houses nestling cosily around a small crescent-shaped harbour. Safiq was tightly enclosed by the mountains, which soared black and sheer directly behind the city. At each end of the bay stood a massive circular fort. Jeannie knew that these had been built by the Portuguese in the sixteenth century, when Portugal ruled this coastal strip—once known as the Pirate Coast and famed for its pearls and black slaves.

She looked out at the harbour, where small high-prowed boats bobbed, ferrying cargoes from the large ships anchored in deep water further out to sea. From their viewpoint on the mountain road, Jeannie could see how clear and shallow the water was. The unbelievable paint-box blue sea glinted alluringly like a brilliant jewel, sparkling its thousand facets back to the sun.

Tarik looked around at her rapturous face. 'Safiq,' he said unnecessarily. 'Too hot for you Europeans.'

'That's not what I was told at the interview,' she said, refusing to be crushed by him.

'I'm not surprised. Safiq is like a woman. Her beauty is on the surface: an illusion. In reality, she has the power to drain you dry and leave you an empty shell.'

'Very cryptic. How on earth can a city do that?' scoffed Jeannie.

'By its climate. There is an ancient Persian saying about the city: "Safiq gives to the panting sinner a taste of the hell to come."'

'You mean it's as hot as Hades?' said Jeannie wryly.

'Exactly. Imagine a daytime temperature of around one hundred degrees. Then imagine those black mountains absorbing all that heat and throwing it back through the night. The place is a natural oven.'

'Safiq's on the coast. That must cool it,' countered Jeannie crisply.

He shook his head. 'India is across that sea. So Safiq receives hot wet winds from the ocean, or hot dry winds from the desert. There's no escape from nature in my country, Miss Bennett, no artificial world to keep you safe from the real one.' He stared hard at her. What did he mean? 'You'll find the humidity is near saturation point,' he added softly.

No escape from nature? Jeannie bit her lip. She was tempted to accuse him of exaggerating but did not dare to provoke another outburst from him. This was probably a further attempt to put her off working here. It certainly didn't feel particularly hot up on the Jafar mountain ridge. Then they jolted down a narrow winding track which abruptly became a tarmac road.

After the emotions of the past few hours, Jeannie was relieved to be entering Safiq. Here at least was a world of well-educated people. She had been assured that the Minister was a cultured man, and she looked forward to a less jarring confrontation with him than she had just experienced. The episode with Tarik was almost over. In only a brief meeting, he had reached a hidden well of passion that she was very anxious to cover up. Such raw emotions were too dangerous to allow to the surface again.

She had seen a television play once about two people who couldn't control their feelings for one another. It had upset her then with its explicit scenes and she had turned it off. Now she was beginning to understand such feelings. How on earth had it ended? she wondered.

Now that they had reached the foot of the mountains, she could reluctantly believe Tarik's description of the heat. It blasted her with its intensity; stifled her with its breathlessness. She sat very still to conserve energy and remain as cool as possible. Out of the corner of her eye she could see that Tarik was sitting forwards, away from the leather back of his seat, and that his hectic driving had slowed considerably.

They turned in through a huge wooden gate in the massive walls, flanked by members of the Sultan's guard who saluted smartly when the Land-Rover hurtled past.

Tarik was forced to drive at a snail's pace in the busy city, especially when he plunged down the narrow alleys. Several times he was confronted with a camel and had to back up into a side turning; it seemed that camels had priority in Safiq.

In a short space of time, they were on the open Colonial-style waterfront which boasted a mere two hundred curving yards of lovely old buildings, their ochre-coloured façades turning pink in the rays of the dying sun. The sea reflected the brilliant reds and oranges of the sky.

Tarik drove slowly along the sea front till they arrived at the hotel where Jeannie half fell out of the back in weariness and relief. A brightly uniformed servant removed her cases and waited for her to follow him up the broad steps. She hesitated, then swung round to look at Tarik, who was watching her with interest.

'If I hear any rumours about me . . .' she said, threateningly.

'I'll say nothing. I'd hate to lose my job, after all.'

Jeannie was sure he was mocking her. She tossed her head.

'See you tomorrow, Miss Bennett.' He sounded resigned.

'I'm not seeing you again,' she said grimly.

'I'm afraid you are. Unless you decide to return home, where you belong.'

Before she could reply, he drove off in a flurry of dust and screeching wheels. Jeannie walked slowly up the steps. She must make absolutely sure that she didn't come into contact with him again.

The hotel was breathtakingly lovely, its Italian lines blending perfectly with the ancient waterfront buildings. The marble steps led to heavy honey-coloured doors, standing open to receive the evening breezes from the Gulf. High above Jeannie's head, the ceiling of the great entrance hall soared in full-bellied curves, depicting the struggle which had given the Sultan's ancestors the position of the ruling family. Slender fluted pillars of gold spread delicate fingers to support the vast ceiling and similar columns formed high traceried archways, framing a vista of massive sandalwood doors at the far end of the hall. Gorgeous tropical plants, huge-leafed and restful, lay banked against the walls and trailed from the upper landing.

In the midst of all this elegance, Jeannie felt dirty and unkempt. She was far too exhausted to hold herself erect and slumped limply through the hall, her trainers squishing noisily on the colourful mosaic floor. The servant leading the way was barefoot and silent. He paused at the reception desk where an immaculate white-robed Riyami welcomed her in English, then preceded her up the grand marble staircase. On the first floor, the walls were hung with red silk, making a vivid background for the dozens of paintings.

Jeannie had lived a very frugal life in puritan surroundings, both at home and then in her own flat. Her mother would have called the hotel decadent; Jeannie thought it was wonderful. And that disturbed her.

She ought to feel uncomfortable in these surroundings. After her father's death, her mother had pared her life to a minimum of contact with others, and a minimum of pleasure. That included Jeannie, too; visitors were discouraged, friends not welcome. Their laughter, their happiness, seemed to upset her mother. Soon Jeannie felt guilty for bringing them and enjoying herself when her mother was so obviously pining. Contact between the two of them became spasmodic, since Jeannie spent most of her spare time studying and her mother worked as a night nurse so that she could afford to put her daughter through university. It was a Spartan, plain life which had been upended by taking this job.

By flying from west to east, it was if she had reversed the way she felt, the way she thought and how she reacted. Here in this exotic and alien country, she was discovering some new and disturbing things about herself.

It made her feel as if she was with a stranger, and it was an uncomfortable feeling. It threw her off balance. Jeannie bit her lip.

All she wanted now was a bath and some sleep. Numbly, she followed the servant down innumerable corridors till he unlocked a door and showed her in. The room was cool and shaded, the sunlight entering only through the slats of huge black shutters. The bed looked large enough for four people and she longed to pad across the marble floor and fling herself down to sleep after the nightmare journey.

A young girl, dressed in a simple yellow robe, rose from a chair, bowed her head and began to unpack the cases, handling the clothes with great interest.

She glanced at Jeannie. 'I am Nava,' she said shyly. 'Said al Saif he say I look after you. You like to wash?'

Jeannie smiled, surprised and a little awkward. 'Oh yes, Nava. I like to wash.'

Nava showed her an ornate marble bathroom leading from the bedroom, and helped Jeannie to run a bath. She poured rich oils into the water, filling the room with powerful haunting fragrances. Jeannie picked up the bottles. One contained frankincense, the other myrrh.

'This one and this one in the bath, make skin nice for man,' said Nava.

Jeannie almost laughed aloud. At the moment, that was one matter farthest from her mind. She stepped into the silken water. It was a good thing she hadn't met Tarik after having a bath here! The perfumes were making her feel languid. It must be the tiredness again. Nava handed her twin soaps.

'This frankincense, this myrrh,' she said.

Jeannie lay back, relaxing in the softly swirling warmth. Saif was doing her proud! The Embassy officials had told her that he had English connections; he was probably eager to impress her. And surely with Saif on her side, Tarik posed no threat. It was unlikely that Saif would listen to his accusations, or any veiled threats.

With the prospect of future comforts and the support of the Minister, she cast aside the events of the day and settled deeper into the caressing, scented water, wondering what Said al Saif looked like. The Minister was really something of a mystery.

Her reverie was startled by the ringing of the telephone on the wall above the bath.

'Hello?' she said uncertainly.

'Miss Bennett?' came an English voice.

'Yes.'

'Hello! I'm Ben Chatsworth—your other half, so to speak. Welcome to Riyam. Journey all right?'

She hesitated. 'Well, I'm a bit tired.'

'I'm sure. Pity the Sultan's planes weren't available. It must have been quite a shock to the bones, traipsing overland like that. Try to reserve judgment about Riyam until you see it in more favourable circumstances.'

Ben sounded a little too friendly so Jeannie tried to inject a little frost in her voice. 'Thank you for your concern. I certainly didn't enjoy the drive much. The forts in the distance seemed interesting, though.'

'Oh, absolutely! Glad you're so positive about things. I'd be pleased to take you round. Saif will probably show you some of the Interior—he took me everywhere when I first arrived, he's nuts about his country. It's marvellous to work for someone who's so enthusiastic. The Interior is his territory, really. You can go anywhere with Saif in perfect safety.'

'But not with you?' asked Jeannie. Despite her initial misgivings, Ben's voice was very disarming.

'Well! There are some bits of the Interior that still hanker after keeping foreigners away.'

'I can believe that,' she said fervently. 'I met someone like that, today.'

'Really? Well, that's unfortunate. Better tell me about it later. 'I've rung to give you the plans for tonight. I suggest you rest for a bit, then I'll meet you in the bar at about nine and we'll get to know each other over dinner, if that's O.K.'

'Sounds lovely,' said Jeannie. 'What's the food like?'

'Cordon bleu stuff. All the oilmen from the Interior come here when they're on leave. And at the oil bases, would you believe, they're used to pheasant, prime steak, smoked salmon and fresh strawberries! The hotel has to keep up to that standard.'

'You're pulling my leg!'

'No, really. Oilmen live in style. Grub is flown in

from all over the world. They don't live like impoverished teachers, you know.'

'Just one thing, Mr Chatsworth,' began Jeannie.

'Oh, please, Ben! And I'd like to call you Jeannie, if I may.'

'Right, Ben. Er . . . what kind of thing do I wear?'

Ben chuckled down the phone. 'I was waiting for that one. The women tend to wear posh frocks—short ones.'

'Thank you. I'll see you later!' Jeannie rang off happily. Everything sounded marvellous. She put the ghastly hours with Tarik out of her mind.

Despite her protests, Nava insisted on drying her, and eventually Jeannie gave up her embarrassed attempts to get dry quickly and luxuriated in the sensation of another person gently massaging her body with a soft towel. Every inch of her skin tingled with sensation, both inside and out, warming to the erotic effect of the exotic oils emanating subtly from every pore.

Jeannie wandered into the bedroom, her skin vibrant, her nose assailed by the fragrance of her body. She slid naked between white silk sheets and slept, dreaming romantic dreams which featured a tall dark Arab with burning eyes and audacious hands.

She was gently shaken awake by Nava. Her body felt hot despite the air-conditioning; the dreams had awoken her senses once more and she squirmed, ashamed at their memory. She contemplated having a cool shower, but Nava seemed anxious about the time. Two dresses were hanging on the outside of the cupboard, both now looking rather plain and demure in the richness of her surroundings. She chose a wild silk grey dress which flowed softly about her body, revealing very little, its neckline just below the collar-bone. The colour complemented her jade eyes and, in fact, proved an attractive contrast to the rather gaudy décor.

Nava brushed out her hair and polished it with a silk cloth, taking pleasure in the gleaming tresses hanging heavily to Jeannie's shoulders. It had been all she could do to prevent Nava from making her face up from the dozens of pots on the dressing table; she merely drew a soft pink lipstick over her lips, staring back at herself in the mirror—an English girl in an Arabian dream! The colour in her cheeks heightened.

Nava smiled in a proprietary way at the lovely heart-shaped face in the mirror. She dabbed minute drops from a tiny phial on to Jeannie's pulse spots and the now familiar aromas of frankincense and myrrh filled the air.

Feeling quite refreshed, with the unpleasant journey behind her, Jeannie made her way to the entrance of the bar and waited, a little uncertainly. A busy throng of people chattered gaily, excluding her from their confident, familiar conversation. A pleasant-faced man rose from the bar and made his way to her, smiling in a friendly way. Jeannie was conscious that the gossiping voices had stopped momentarily and that everyone was staring at her. She lowered her head, a little disconcerted by their interest.

'Hey! Don't do that! Don't spoil our view!' Ben Chatsworth shook her hand and led her to the bar, ordering drinks for them both. She estimated that Ben was in his mid-thirties. With his brown wavy hair, medium height and slender build, he would hardly have stood out in a crowd but Jeannie was immediately drawn to the kindness in his eyes and the welcome of his smile. It was a relief to have a possible ally.

'At the risk of your thinking I'm "on the make", I'm going to tell you that you look great. At last Safiq has something new to talk about!' She couldn't take offence at his tone. But she blushed, nevertheless.

'I wish I didn't keep doing that,' she murmured, feeling the pink colour steal into her soft gold cheeks.

'Many women would give five years of their life to be the kind of girl who blushes,' he said quietly. 'Don't worry about it. It says a lot about you.'

'It shouldn't. I'm not really the blushing sort. Tell me all about what I'm to do,' she said, quickly changing the subject.

'You are keen!'

'I have one or two people to convince.'

Ben smiled. 'Well, I'm convinced—I've seen your curriculum vitae. And now I've seen you, well!'

Thanks heavens he was a safe man!

'Thank you, Ben. You don't know how unsure I've been of myself over these last few days.'

'Quite unnecessary but very natural, after being swept into another *century*, let alone another country,' he replied. 'It's an extraordinary place, Riyam. You'll love it. Absolutely teeming with interest. Terrific picnics we have at night, you know, on the beach, watching the crabs pop out of the sand. Then there's Hayda, that's a crusader fort, and . . . Oh, I could go on all night. I'd better not wear you out now, though. We'll take things easy to start with. You need to adjust to the heat. In most of the government buildings we have air conditioning, but you have to venture out sometimes!'

'The heat does worry me,' murmured Jeannie.

'You soon acclimatise if you remember a few rules. Don't ever rush, don't ever get angry. Not much to make anyone cross here, anyway! Take advantage of the long breaks in work to nip back and have a shower—that's what we all do here, you know. You'll be at the hotel till we get you settled in a flat. Any problems, come to me. We want to make things go as smoothly as possible.'

His words reassured her even further. 'I'm going to like working with you.'

He grinned. 'Looks as though we'll get on—that's great. It's such a close community here, good relationships are important. Now, what first? If we take each day as it comes for a while... Um, tomorrow morning I've been detailed to introduce you to the Education Minister.'

'Oh good! I've been looking forward to meeting him.'

'He's a great bloke. One of the most powerful men in the country. We're really lucky to be working for him. The tribesmen think the world of him—and it takes a lot to win their respect. They're not influenced by money or position, only quality.'

'What a relief. I hate working for inadequate people,' said Jeannie. Things were looking up. It seemed that the awful Tarik was not typical of the Riyamis.

'Nothing inadequate about him, I can assure you. Makes me feel positively puny, though. One word of warning; watch your step as far as his pride is concerned—be tactful. He can be very touchy if he thinks you're acting like our overbearing Victorian ancestors. Go easy on the empire-building bit. And for heaven's sake, don't imply the people here are ignorant.'

Jeannie looked shocked—as if she would! Even the insufferable Tarik had shown that he could navigate in a featureless desert. Ought she to tell Ben about him? It worried her that Tarik might assault another woman and it would be her fault if she was too embarrassed to expose his behaviour. And the trouble was, he knew how she'd felt for a few moments; she might deny it, but she was a poor liar. Damn him! He deserved to be sacked. She supposed she ought to keep her side of the bargain. If only he could be relied on to keep his!

She was sipping her drink rapidly when their waiter announced that their table was ready. The walk to the dining room was unnerving; Jeannie felt as if she was on display.

'Do they always stare at new people?' she whispered to Ben.

'No! You've set Safiq about the ears!' he grinned.

Jeannie frowned slightly. She'd seen the admiration in the men's eyes and imagined it must be because there were so few women around. She had no idea that the episode in the oasis had affected the way she looked; what was once a frigid and indrawn look was now one of awakening discovery of her own sensuality. She was giving out glowing vibrations. Tarik's passion had stirred her more deeply than she knew. Every man there recognised the latent blooming of womanhood within her; the women envied the beauty that sprang from her arousal.

At the moment she was too preoccupied to be aware of the dramatic change in the way she walked, the movements of her body and the expression in her eyes. Innocently, she carried the signs of a yearning woman while still lacking any knowledge of her own potential fascination.

'It's not often anyone turns up looking like you,' continued Ben.

'I can see you're headed for the diplomatic corps,' said Jeannie wryly. She hoped he wouldn't get too friendly. That was the last thing she wanted.

'Huh! I should be so lucky. Look, I don't want to sound as if I'm telling tales out of school, but . . . well, I think you ought to know. If you looked like the back of a bus I wouldn't bother, but Saif is quite a ladies' man. One of those good-lookers with one hell of a smooth reputation. Money, power, fantastic physique—why can't things be shared out more equally?' Ben looked pleadingly at Jeannie, as though she might help.

She giggled. 'Let's get one thing clear straight away: I positively don't want any entanglements. I've just got out of one. The Minister can't be that gorgeous, Ben, or he'd have been snapped up. Or is he married and still playing the field?'

'I'm not sure. It's difficult to say. I gather there is some woman around, but I don't know if they're married. He keeps his affairs very secret. If he is married, it hasn't stopped the nurses in the local hospital from angling for him. I gather there's a world market in bleeding hearts at Casualty! So, if you want to keep your reputation and heart intact, be careful. You're . . .' He looked into her wide and newly vulnerable eyes. 'Well, just don't let him hurt you, that's all. I'd hate to have you weeping on my shoulder! No, wait, what am I saying? It would be rather nice!'

Jeannie laughed. 'Don't worry, Ben. There's no likelihood of my turning emotional. I intend to work here, not get entangled with a Casanova type.'

'That's a relief. A beautiful and sensible woman! I can hardly believe my luck. Don't be put off by what I've told you. You'll find him a very fair man, and completely objective.'

As Ben had promised, the dinner was superb. Jeannie sipped a very dry white wine and rejoiced in her good luck. Ben would be easy to get on with, straightforward and pleasant. She wouldn't need any barriers against him. Tarik would be laughing on the other side of his face when she signed up at the end of the three months, for a five-year contract.

'Coffee in the lounge, I think,' announced Ben.

Jeannie sank into the plump red cushions, a perfect foil for her dress and delicate features.

'I heard the Minister couldn't meet you at Fallah. Pity that, he's terrific on a journey—full of info. about the area. Hope the replacement driver was O.K.?'

Jeannie hesitated long enough for Ben to become suspicious.

'Some kind of problem?' he asked.

'A bit.' She lowered her eyes. 'It was so tedious and so long, of course, especially from Fallah to Safiq . . .'

'You've got it wrong. That bit is a doddle. What time did you leave Fallah?'

'Well, late last night.'

'And when did you arrive in Safiq?'

'About sunset.' She was startled by his reaction.

'Never! What on earth did you do all the time?'

She frowned. What did he mean? Had he heard something from Tarik? 'We drove, of course,' she said sharply.

'Jeannie, Safiq is only a few hours' drive from Fallah. You should have arrived before coffee time! Where the hell did you go? Did you stop to sightsee? If not, the man must have taken an extraordinarily roundabout route!'

'We drove for most of the time. I . . . I did think we were going westwards at one stage,' she said.

'Westwards! What can he have been playing at? All the drivers in the department know this area like the back of their hands. What was his name, do you know?'

'Please, Ben, I don't want any trouble,' said Jeannie nervously.

'Trouble! I'll give him trouble! No wonder it seemed a long journey! You must be shattered. Did anything else happen? He didn't try anything on, did he?'

'Well, the Land-Rover got stuck in the sand,' she said, 'but that can't have been his fault.'

Ben puckered his forehead. 'Doesn't sound like one of our men at all; none of them would do anything so stupid. It would take an idiot to come off the trail into soft sand. I think I'd better do a bit of investigating. What did you say his name was?'

'Ben, please don't start my duty here with a row. The man made mistakes. I'm asking you as a favour, don't make waves.'

She was really worried now. Tarik would be unscrupulous enough to spread stories about her surrender to him in the pool if Ben made trouble.

'It's very nice of you, Jeannie, but I'll find out, whether you want me to or not. Look, I appreciate your motives. Tell you what, let me know his name and I promise faithfully I won't make any fuss at all— I won't even mention anything to the man. All I want to do is to ensure that no one has to go through such a chaotic journey as you did. That's fair, isn't it? You can trust me. I must say, to have travelled for nearly twenty-four hours unnecessarily and then not make a fuss seems to be extraordinarily generous of you.'

Jeannie hated Ben to think so well of her when she was really trying to hide her guilty secret. She decided she could trust him.

'He was pretty foul. He said he was some sort of clerk in the department; Tarik, he called himself. Is it possible for me not to have much contact with him? He was really rather objectionable.'

'Tarik! But we don't have a Tarik. Said al Saif must have borrowed him from some other department. You needn't worry, it doesn't look as though you'll meet him again.'

So Tarik had been lying, after all. And from what

Ben said, it seemed as if he had deliberately driven around in circles to make the journey a trying one for her, hoping that she would decide to go back to England! What a foul thing to do! Even the trouble with the Land-Rover could have been merely a ploy.

And could his attempted seduction of her have been some kind of twisted means to frighten her off? He'd carefully calculated his actions, knowing that his highly experienced technique would affect her. The swine! She hated people who lied and played games for their own ends. Now Jeannie felt even more deeply ashamed of her reactions. He must have been vastly amused by it! She had confirmed all his prejudices about British women. What a relief that he had nothing to do with the department. His parting words had been empty threats, after all.

After coffee, Ben escorted her to her room, worried that she would be worn out from travelling solidly for the past two days.

'I'll pick you up at eight tomorrow morning, in the entrance hall,' he said.

'Eight! Are you serious!' she cried.

''Fraid so. You see, we were expecting you to have spent today resting. That fellow Tarik has a lot to answer for. I can't change the appointment, though I understand how weary you must be. We've a meeting with Saif at eight-fifteen and no one mucks him about—or if they do, they only do it once!

'Everyone starts work early here, because of the heat, you know. Our normal hours are eight to eleven, then three to eight, with half-hour breaks whenever you choose for refreshment. Apart from the meeting with Saif, we'll take it easy on you tomorrow.'

'So long as I don't have to see another Land-Rover for a while!' she laughed.

'I promise! Sleep well, and see you eight o'clock.'

CHAPTER FOUR

BY eight-ten the next morning, they were in the Minister's personal reception room, overlooking the harbour. Thick golden carpets cushioned their feet and huge paradise palms were grouped with colourful hibiscus plants in elegant ceramic pots. Looking around the light and airy room, Jeannie decided that money was obviously no object. A battery of telephones lay on the secretary's desk and he was constantly stretching from one instrument to another, apologising for Saif's absence in English and Arabic.

Ben looked up as they heard a low whirring noise.

'Saif's private lift,' he murmured to Jeannie.

She waited for the Minister to appear, but there was no sign of him so she looked questioningly at Ben.

'Oh!' he smiled at her puzzled face. 'The lift takes him directly to his office. Very useful for welcome and unwelcome visitors. He can escape from, or with, whoever he chooses!'

The Minister was definitely an intriguing man, thought Jeannie. There was a long buzz on an intercom and the secretary disappeared through the heavy sandalwood door labelled 'Education Minister: HH Said al Saif'. A deep voice could be heard behind it, harsh and angry. The door opened and Saif's secretary invited them inside.

Jeannie walked carefully on the thick cream carpet, trying not to catch her small heels in the deep pile. The Minister's office was more like a drawing room than a place of business, with its carefully arranged easy chairs for discussion, its small brass-topped coffee tables, the thin cream curtains at the full-length windows and the oil paintings of desert scenes. Massive banks of greenery relieved the pale peach walls and would have added to the impression of peace if it had not been dispelled by the taut atmosphere within the room.

For the surroundings were imprinted only fleetingly on Jeannie's mind. The tension emanated from the Minister, standing with his back to them, staring through a huge floor-length plate glass window at the Gulf of Riyam, spread, dazzling and sparkling, far below. The set of his body predicted a furious and daunting man, even his broad back portraying a compelling figure used to authority.

He was very tall and much younger than she had imagined earlier. The power in his shoulders could be recognised under his expertly tailored pin-striped suit, and the white collar of his shirt emphasised the bronze of his neck and the blackness of his hair. Tanned brown hands were clenched hard on his hips, flaring out the jacket above tight trousers, cut to reveal the line of his taut muscular legs straddled aggressively apart.

Jeannie felt a little in awe of him already. Such an urbane-looking back! Automatically, she ran her fingers through her hair and immediately wished she hadn't. She didn't seem to know what to do with her hands—they felt awkward and huge. The air of wealth surrounding him, the deference shown by Ben's hesitant manner, and the poised strength of the Minister, all served to make her feel very young and inexperienced.

'Said al Saif?' murmured Ben politely.

The Minister swung round, his face as dark as thunder. And in that moment, Jeannie's hopes of a marvellous new career were completely dashed. Said al

Saif, Ben had said. Impossible, unbelievable, but it was Tarik standing there!

She held her breath. Ben was introducing her, telling her that this was the Minister. Tarik's double, maybe? There couldn't be two of him, surely? As he glared at her, she knew it was the same man who had fought to possess the fourteen-year-old girl, who had forced her to undergo a gruelling and unnecessary journey in the desert, who had pretended the Land-Rover was overheated and then stuck in the sand. He was the same man who had trailed his hands so sensuously over her body, kissed her so expertly and awakened sensations which even now refused to be subdued. At the sight of him, a rush of fevered heat forced itself through her body, scattering all rational thought.

Jeannie fought for clear-headedness. She had made a worse mess of things than she had originally imagined. And Tarik patently wanted her to leave Riyam. What price her career now!

Her hands shook in anger, her nervousness totally forgotten at this discovery of an idol with feet of clay. But while she stared back with scarcely veiled contempt, she was realising that the Minister was no longer someone she could look to for protection. In a few seconds he had turned into the most despicable man she had ever met. What would he do to her?

Saif's chest rose against the constricting formal suit. Gone was the tousled-looking ruffian. Now a suave, rich man stood before her, flashing a heavy gold watch and cuff links at his strong wrists. Since the suit fitted as if it was virtually a second skin, no doubt it had cost a fortune, along with the soft black leather shoes that looked as if an army of servants had spent a whole morning polishing them. Divested of his simple Arab robes, he took on an air of authority and sophistication which, coupled with his dramatic looks, would have set any woman's pulses racing.

Jeannie's were racing for other reasons. Would he now denounce her? Was this behaviour some kind of test that she had abysmally failed? A succession of pink flushes tinged her face. Tarik's eyes were on her face now, his cynical eyes running over her clear forehead with its wisps of golden curls which had escaped from the once-smooth hair, resting on the arching mouth and small determined chin.

She couldn't tear her eyes away from him. When his gaze lingered on her soft mouth, it was impossible for her to stop her lips from parting. As she moistened them with the tip of her tongue, his mocking eyes met hers for one brief moment then swept down across her body with a cursory glance, as if she was an uninteresting object for sale.

It was all so unfair. With this man's hatred ahead of her, she was doomed. If only she had taken his advice! She would have done better to return on the next plane before she met 'Tarik' again in the form of the 'illustrious' Minister. What must he think of her?

She pulled herself together and waited for the scornful denunciation. But none came. The introduction was over and Saif was bowing curtly. He gave no Arab greeting, nor did he offer his hand, Western-style.

'How do you do?' he said harshly, masking his dislike with obvious difficulty.

'How—how do you do?' whispered an appalled Jeannie.

There was an awkward silence. Ben turned from one to the other in concern. Then the Minister startled Jeannie by striding past them and opening the door. For one moment she thought he was intending to demand that she should leave, and it was with a feeling

of relief that she heard him speak in clipped tones to
the secretary.

'Jahn, please turn up the air conditioning. I'm
thinking Miss Bennett is finding the climate in Safiq
too torrid.'

She flushed at the double meaning of his words and
miserably lifted her chin, looking stonily ahead. So he
was pretending not to know her! She was more than
prepared to go along with that. But what a mean trick
to play on her, pretending he was some unimportant
clerk! How he must be laughing at her gullibility—
and, worse, how he must be congratulating himself on
adding yet another female to his list of conquests. She
had been very silly. Giving in to emotions was always
a mistake. It mustn't happen again. This man's
behaviour had put her on her guard against any
further attempts.

'Miss Bennett?' came his curt voice.

'I'm sorry. What...?' Darn him, she'd missed
what he'd said.

'The Said wondered whether you would like some
coffee, Jeannie,' said Ben, his eyes anxiously on her.

'Yes, please,' she said quietly.

'Is anything the matter, sir?' asked Ben. Said al
Saif's barely controlled anger was worrying him.
Normally he was so gracious to visitors. He hoped that
Jeannie wasn't thinking that Saif was an uncivilised
boor. Ben didn't want him to appear in a bad light to
her.

'I'm sorry, Ben.' Saif's manner relaxed slightly.
'I've had some difficulties at home. That's why I am
so late—and not a little bad-tempered. Please forgive
me, I dislike unpunctuality in others, and it seems the
height of rudeness to be late myself.'

'A very smooth lie of Tarik's—or rather Saif's,'
thought Jeannie. 'He's just trying to cover up his

dislike of me.' She was proved wrong, however, by a telephone call which Saif took on his personal phone, first excusing himself and carrying the instrument over to the window.

'Yes?' he barked. He listened to a long tirade, audible even from across the room. 'You'll have to cope. I'm in a meeting. What? Hell! The child is your responsibility. Then get anything else breakable out of his way. Mahine, for the love of Allah, let me get on with my job! . . . All right . . . No, I'm out for dinner.'

He listened to another tirade, his embarrassed glance flickering over Ben and Jeannie who pretended not to be listening. 'Late. After you've gone to bed. No. Send him to bed at his usual time. There's no point in either of you waiting up. Mahine, I'll discuss it over breakfast, not now. I must go.'

He slammed down the receiver, his temper not improved in the least. It sounded as though he was having problems after all, and that must have been his wife, Jeannie supposed. Poor woman, she probably waited at home many a time while he entertained girl friends.

Jeannie decided she didn't like Saif one bit. He thought too much of himself and had a callous disregard for anyone's feelings. Looking at him in his European clothes, so mature and worldly, she felt scorn for the role he had effected as a tough tribesman. He was obviously an inveterate liar.

Tarik, indeed! No doubt he used that name for his nefarious activities. She wondered how many other women had been insulted or misled as she had. It seemed that Saif was a chameleon; ready to use abuse, deviant tricks, or seduction to gain power over people and achieve his own ends. Jeannie hardened her heart to him and sharpened her wits, ready to do battle. The man would discover he had met his match!

'I do apologise for the interruption.' Saif smiled with his lips, not his eyes which were still blazing furiously. 'Please sit down.'

Jeannie sank into a soft armchair, leaning back and looking as relaxed as she could. Tarik sat opposite, hard and uncompromising, watching her every move. The silk of her dress whispered softly as she tried to get comfortable under his scrutiny.

Behind her, the door opened and the secretary brought in a tray of coffee and small biscuits. Judging from the strain on Jahn's face as he carried the tray, the large coffee jug was pure silver. Saif certainly knew how to look after himself.

'Black and strong, or pale and weak?' asked Saif innocently.

'In between, please,' replied Jeannie firmly. Round one to me, she thought. 'I don't care for extremes.'

'Then you will not be happy here. Riyam is a country of extremes.'

'So I've discovered,' she said.

'Not having second thoughts already, Miss Bennett?'

'No, I think my qualifications are suitable. I should be able to handle . . . everything.' Her meaning was clear to him; he allowed himself a small smile. She was beginning to enjoy herself.

'I hope you find the hotel comfortable.'

'Yes, thank you.' She tried to sound as natural as possible for Ben's sake—he must have noticed the air of tension in the room.

'Your flat is not quite ready. I'm sure you are looking forward to being . . . ah . . . independent.'

'You're darn right I am!' she said to herself.

'I can see you understand Western women, Minister,' she answered sweetly. 'I'm not quite clear about Nava, though. She's a wonderful maid and it was very good of you to be considerate, but I don't think I can afford her.'

'A maid?' Ben was astonished.

'Nava has asked to be your—ah—maid,' said Saif, ignoring Ben, 'to improve her English. Please speak to her in return for the work she does. That will be payment enough.'

'I'm not used . . .' began Jeannie, but was silenced by Saif's frown and Ben's warning look.

'It would offend me if you turned her out. It would almost certainly upset her. You will keep her, therefore. Since she will cost you nothing, you can hardly object.'

His words sounded final. Jeannie wondered why he'd engaged Nava. The only reason she could think of was that he was trying to spy on her. It seemed unbelievable that he could stoop so low, but then it was unbelievable that this man had already behaved so badly. She'd love to find out why he'd taken such a dislike to her.

'Was the weather in England pleasant when you left?' continued Saif.

'Delightful,' said Jeannie mockingly. The conversation was becoming ridiculous.

'Good. Perhaps, Miss Bennett, with your permission, we may now turn to business?' At her nod, he addressed Ben.

'Before we discuss Miss Bennett's role, I want to take this opportunity to check our priorities. The most urgent matter, of course, is to complete arrangements for the school in southern Nafud. Can you give an opening date? The Sultan is becoming a little impatient, and the Sheikh of Nafud feels insulted by the delay.'

'Yes, sir. I appreciate his concern. However, I did explain to him that the teachers from Britain had to complete their present contracts before they could be released and make their way to this country. I visited him yesterday and reassured him that we weren't prepared to settle merely for adequately qualified staff. For his school, we were insisting on the best. That did mollify him.'

The Minister grinned broadly, his face relaxing into almost pleasant lines. 'You are becoming more Arab than the Arabs with your flattery, Ben. So, what is the position now?'

'As you know, the building is ready and the equipment is ready to leave Abu Dhabi. The two members of staff are flying in from London next week and we hope they can begin sometime during the week after that, but I'm afraid I can't give you the exact day. It rather depends on all those factors coming good,' said Ben.

'And with the two additional Riyami teachers, the school will definitely be able to take every child in the south?'

'Yes sir, with room and teacher/pupil ratios to spare.'

'Excellent. I want you to send word to the Riyami staff to prepare the school and begin the mother tongue curriculum. Let them know that I intend to visit it—' he consulted his diary and scribbled furiously for a moment '—on Thursday. We can iron out any problems then.'

'Yes sir. And with the south of the city provided for, what about the north? Logically we should provide a school in upper Nafud next, but I see on your priorities sheet that it's way down on the list. I think we'll have trouble with them if they're not due to have a school for another year or so.'

'They're not ready for a school. Give it time.'

Jeannie had been following the conversation carefully and couldn't help interrupting. She leaned forward and asked: 'Excuse me, Minister. Could you explain how you determined which were the priority areas? Did you take into account the needs of the people, or did you have other criteria?'

'Meaning?' Saif was frowning.

'I'm not quite clear why one part of a town is ready for a school and another part isn't.' I bet it's bribery, she thought.

'I take all factors into account, Miss Bennett. They are far too complicated to explain now. In time, you will discover the complexities. For now, you'll have to trust my judgment.'

'Do you ever make a mistake, sir?' she asked sweetly.

His hands clenched. 'No!'

'So half the town has a school and the other half doesn't.'

'Right.'

'And just when will the school be built in the north, Minister?'

'When I decide the time is right, and not before. This matter doesn't concern you. I do not wish to discuss it any further.'

Again his word was final. Ben made no attempt to challenge the decision. Was he intimidated by al Saif? It worried Jeannie a little that he was so pliant. If she ever had to cross Saif, she would have to do it alone.

'I would like you to show Miss Bennett how the Nafud school was set up,' said Saif. 'Give her every detail. Once she has a clear idea, then I want her to start on her own—perhaps next week.'

Ben's mouth dropped open in amazement. 'Next week! Sir, may I suggest that we ease Miss Bennett in more gently? It's perfectly possible, if you're in agreement, for her to go through a couple of operations with me first,' he said. 'But it's rather early days for her to be branching out on her own, you know. It took me six months before I knew the ropes.'

'That's irrelevant. We haven't time to carry passengers, there's too much to do. Everyone has to pull their own weight. I'm accelerating the programme.'

Jeannie crossed her legs, provoking a cold glance from Saif.

'I had it on good authority that Riyamis hated rapid change,' she said coolly.

'They all want schools,' growled Saif.

'Even in Nafud?' retorted Jeannie.

Saif banged down his cup. She'd needled him; good!

Ben was signalling something to Jeannie; he seemed very agitated. To hell with that, she wasn't going to let up on Saif; she probably knew him better than Ben.

'Shall we see how things go, sir?' asked Ben desperately.

'No, we won't. Miss Bennett is a very clever woman.' He fixed Jeannie with his penetrating eyes. 'Or so various people have told me. When you arrived, you were working blind, Ben; she has you to guide her. These projects are urgent. We can't hold them up. You can't work together, that's a waste of resources. Besides, I want you to fly to Sheddah soon and work there for a few months. Miss Bennett can handle things at the Safiq end.'

They were discussing her as if she was not there. It irked Jeannie that they never considered consulting her for her own views on the matter.

'Of course, sir. But if I go to Sheddah, I can't guide Miss Bennett, not at a distance, you know!' Ben sat on the edge of his chair, his hands twisting together in consternation. 'No disrespect to Miss Bennett, but if I left, it would put the whole programme in jeopardy. I respect your needs, sir, but the pressure on Miss Bennett would be unfair. Of course, if this is the

Sultan's request, I'm willing to explain to him why it's not a good idea, if you like. He can't reasonably expect her to cope unsupported.'

'It is *my* decision, not the Sultan's. I want you in Sheddah as soon as possible.'

'I'm sure I can manage,' Jeannie said confidently.

Ben and Saif turned in surprise. They had obviously forgotten her.

Ben cleared his throat. 'Sir, you know how difficult the sheikhs can be. I'd be much happier if . . .'

'From her file, and from other more intimate sources, I hear that Miss Bennett is extremely efficient and organised,' interrupted Saif. His hand rested on a folder and Jeannie recognised the awful photograph she'd had taken on the front of it. For the interview and the photo session, she'd scraped back her hair in an unbecoming bun in an effort to look as responsible and serious as possible.

'With your briefing,' continued Saif, 'I am sure she will be delighted to take on the local sheikhs. If there are problems—well, Miss Bennett will do her best, I'm sure.' He smiled beguilingly at Jeannie.

'I know what your game is!' she thought bitterly. 'You're deliberately putting me in a position where I'll be bound to make mistakes.'

She pursed her lips, before saying, 'My best will be more than good enough, Minister. In any case, I can always rely on the department for assistance, can't I?'

The corners of the Minister's mouth lifted wryly and he bent his head to acknowledge that she was playing the game of cat and mouse very well.

'Since you both have much to do, I am sure you wish to get started,' he said, leaning back in dismissal. Ben and Jeannie rose and made for the door. 'One moment, Miss Bennett,' called Saif. She turned. 'The glowing references to certain qualities in here,' he tapped the file again, 'speak highly of your organisational abilities and your natural authority. But what may be appropriate back in England is not necessarily appropriate here.'

'I don't understand,' said Jeannie.

'An assertive nature in a woman is a disadvantage in Riyam. You would do well to study how Ben queries decisions rather than openly opposing them. Don't argue with men. It won't get you anywhere.'

'You don't want me to question anything?'

'Not in the tone you used today, no.'

'So I am to be meek and submissive?' Jeannie's tone was ominous.

'I'm afraid that would be too much to hope for, from you. That's hardly your style. However, I think there are ways a woman can put her point of view and still make an impact.'

'So I've heard, Minister.' Did he mean the wide-eyed approach, or the casting couch method, she wondered?

'So, develop subtlety. The sheikhs will expect it. Oh, and two more things.' His eyes burned into hers. 'I think you should tie back your hair. It will be cooler if you do so, and less . . . ah . . . abandoned. Also—' he sniffed delicately '—your perfume is perfect for a bedroom seduction, but not for office hours, and certainly not for meeting the sheikhs. Please don't wear it again to work.' He gave a curt, dismissive nod and turned his back on her.

Jeannie let out a gasp of disbelief. Ben quickly touched her arm, aware of her shock. He was surprised himself at Saif's words. He sensed she was about to retort and quickly forestalled her.

'We'll be going now then, sir. I'll keep you up to date on Nafud. Goodbye, sir,' he said rapidly, propelling Jeannie to the door.

'Well!' she breathed once they were outside.

'Don't say anything for a moment,' said Ben. 'You might regret it.' He took Jeannie's shaking arm. 'Look, I think we'd better have a sit by the harbour wall for a few minutes. You look all chewed up.'

Too astonished—and angry—to speak, Jeannie followed, holding herself tightly in check. Her mind was in a turmoil from the meeting. She sat with Ben on the wall, staring out at the harbour, seeing nothing.

'I've never known such an extraordinary morning!' said Ben finally. 'Things have really started to hum now you've arrived! And heaven knows what's come over Saif.'

When Jeannie made no response, apart from chewing her lip angrily, he continued: 'Look, Jeannie, about the advice he gave you; it was meant in good faith. I think he was only trying to help you, so that you didn't upset any Riyami officials you might deal with—or even tribesmen, when you begin to bargain for buildings in towns.

'And, well, he was probably a bit worried about your forthright manner. He's got some rather fixed ideas about women, I'm afraid. In fact, it's all my fault in a way. I should have suggested you tone down your attractions a bit, but—well—it seemed rude. The Minister had the guts to do so. I hadn't.'

'He doesn't mind being insolent, you mean.'

'No, Jeannie. He's trying to make things go smoothly. If I'd thought, I would have said the same thing.'

'But not in those words. He implied I was trying to be seductive.' Jeannie pushed back her thick hair, still fuming from Saif's remarks.

'No, I'm sure he wasn't. But he's much more honest than I am, he goes straight to the point—very unusual for an Arab. But then, he had an English mother so that might explain it.'

'It does!' exclaimed Jeannie. 'His perfect English, I mean.'

'Oh, well, he was educated in some public school in the south of England. He wasn't taught any English by his mother; apparently she was a bit of a good-time girl. She abandoned him and his brother Ahmed when they were tiny, and his father died soon after. It was quite a while ago—something like twenty-five years, I think—but Saif's never forgiven or forgotten. The story goes that the two boys were left to beg in the streets of Muscat. No welfare state here, you see.'

'But surely the Minister is related to the Sultan,' said Jeannie, puzzled.

'Distantly. The problem was that Saif's father had already isolated himself by marrying a European. It took some while before anyone dared to suggest that the Sultan should help the boys.'

'Bit of a tough start to life,' said Jeannie, her thoughts turning to the loss of her own parents.

'I should think it was one hell of a shock, finding you have no mother, father, or home. Now you see why he's got a chip on his shoulder about English-women—and a funny attitude to women anyway. A bit defensive.'

'You can say that again,' said Jeannie. 'That doesn't excuse his rudeness, though.'

'No, he did go a bit over the top today. He's not usually like that, honestly. Don't prejudge him. He was obviously having awful problems at home. Sounds as if the woman on the end of the phone couldn't cope with his kiddie.'

Jeannie started. She had been so preoccupied with his criticisms of her that she had forgotten about the woman.

'She seemed very agitated,' she said slowly.

'His wife, I suppose,' agreed Ben.

'That's what I thought. Well, my sympathies are all with her. It seems that their son has inherited a fiery temper from his father.'

'Now, Jeannie,' reproved Ben. 'You're not listening to me. He's very rarely like this. In fact, the last time was when his brother Ahmed surprised everyone by marrying one of the English typists from Saif's office.'

'Wow!' grinned Jeannie. 'I can imagine the fuss *that* must have caused.'

'He was right to be angry. She was a real gold-digger—left Ahmed suddenly a couple of years ago and skipped back to Southampton to cook up her divorce settlement. It's common knowledge that Ahmed has hardly stopped drinking since then.'

'The Saifs haven't had much luck with my countrywomen, have they?' murmured Jeannie.

She was going to have rather an uphill struggle to make any kind of working relationship with her employer. Perhaps, in a few days, she would be able to assess whether it was worthwhile bothering. 'What about the rest of his family?' She was suddenly very curious.

'Shrouded in even greater mystery. He keeps them totally in the background, you know. None of them appear in public, not even to any functions or celebrations. I've honestly never seen this Mahine, or his son.'

'If you ask me, he's a dyed-in-the-wool Arab who keeps his wife under wraps,' said Jeannie. 'For the sake of *my* temper, let alone his, I intend to keep out of his way for a while. I only hope he can control his vindictiveness the next time we meet.'

'Please, Jeannie. You're talking about my boss, and

yours. You're also talking about the man I most admire, so be careful.'

Jeannie's opinion of Ben took a nose-dive. She tackled him on the matter which had worried her earlier.

'When you disagreed with him about the school in Nafud, he brushed your opinion aside and insisted he was right,' she said. 'Does he always do that?'

'Yes and no. Most of the time he listens politely and explains carefully why your ideas won't work. He's usually immaculately polite and thoughtful—like the way he made conversation before we began to discuss business. Arabs hate launching straight into business, they think it's bad manners. Remember that, Jeannie. Usually they spend ten minutes gossiping before coming to the purpose of a meeting. Anyway, this time he was too short-tempered to explain why the school is a low priority. He'll tell me next time, I'm sure.'

'What about sending you off and leaving me to pick up the threads here, then?' demanded Jeannie. She wasn't going to let Ben get away with that one. He had been even more shocked than she was by the idea.

He grinned ruefully. 'Yes, that's extraordinary. Again, all I can say is that I respect his judgment. There's bound to be a good reason. He knows things I don't.'

'You put a lot of trust in him, don't you?' she said.

'We all do, Jeannie. It's a well-deserved trust. You'll soon find that out. As I said, something's happened to knock him off balance.'

'Yes, me,' thought Jeannie. 'Well, I'm glad I've got under his skin. I'm glad my presence in his precious country annoys him. I intend to annoy him even more by being a success at my job.'

Ben was patting her hand. 'What a hell of an

introduction you've had! From now on it can only get better. If you feel O.K. now, we'll have a look at the school here to give you an idea of what we're aiming at. Then we'll go over the work for the Nafud site. You have a planning meeting with the Minister this evening at six. We'll check later with his secretary to see if he can still make it. Heaven knows what's happening at his home.'

Jeannie tried hard to shrug off the upsetting beginning to her morning. Ben took her to the tiny, two-roomed school just behind the waterfront, which was one of six similar schools in Safiq. With great determination, she flung herself into the morning's work and was surprised when Ben told her it was time to leave the little school.

'Come tomorrow?' asked a little girl, her huge dark eyes pleading with Jeannie.

'I will come again,' said Jeannie, writing it on the child's slate. The child ran to her Riyami teacher who smiled and translated, leading all the children to the school entrance so they could wave goodbye.

'You made a good impression,' said Ben.

'I surprised myself, actually,' said Jeannie. 'What is it about these people that I like so much—with one or two exceptions, of course?'

'They've got a lot of old-fashioned standards of behaviour. Many of them are descended from the great Bedouin tribes. For them, a man's response to other men is infinitely more important than his position in the world. They respect age, so the children wouldn't dream of being impolite to adults. All adults, whatever their rank, defer to their elders.'

'So someone like Saif would feel respect for an older man, however unimportant?' asked Jeannie.

'That's right.'

'I see. I noticed how gentle and kind the teacher

was. When you're appointing teachers, do you look for qualities like that as well as qualifications?'

'You've got it! It's most important in this country; there are such strong social courtesies. You're beginning to get the flavour of Riyam already. Talking of flavours, I'll buy you a sherbet in the hotel and then you must rest in your room. The heat must be getting too much for you.'

Ben rang the Minister's office at six and Jeannie was relieved to hear that Saif was still at home and unable to keep his appointment with her. For the next few days, she worked hard with Ben, gradually acclimatising herself and swinging into a steady routine. Each night, though, she slept badly, tossing after her bath, unable to quiet her throbbing pulses. Each day she flung herself into her work with determination, hoping to forget the emptiness that surrounded all her quiet moments. In her own mind, she had dismissed the longing to feel Tarik's arms around her once more, but her body refused to forget. She felt as if her physical needs were getting out of control and worked feverishly to quell the emotions which kept rising to the surface.

Perhaps it was being so far from home that made her lonely. Whatever the reason, she felt empty and incomplete, longing for someone to confide in, to take an interest in the things she was doing.

That week, Ben introduced her to many of his friends who made her very welcome. But she was nervous of her new, vulnerable state. Evenings were spent fending off hopeful men or avoiding confidences from the women. They all wanted to know everything about her and she wasn't prepared to expose herself to all that well-meant interest. Luckily, the daily work-load increased to such an extent that she often worked through the evenings. Work became a convenient excuse to avoid invitations.

Saif was responsible for the extra work. Frequent memos arrived on her desk, requesting information or sending her on long fruitless journeys to negotiate for building plots. Jeannie refused to weaken in her determination to show Saif that she was capable.

When a local trader finally agreed to sell the Ministry a particularly good site for a school, she was delighted with her early success. Hurrying excitedly down the corridor on her way to show Ben the plans, she bumped right into the Minister.

'Hell!' he swore. She'd knocked a cup out of his hand. His once-immaculate stone-coloured suit and her white dress were splashed with coffee stains.

'I'm sorry! I'll get you another,' she cried.

'Suit?' he growled.

'Coffee.' In the wrong again!

'Don't bother. It was cold anyway. Come to my office.' He turned on his heel and left her staring after him. Sighing at his high-handed order, she reluctantly followed.

'Where are you?' His voice came from behind a narrow doorway. 'Come in.'

She walked into a black marbled wash-room, her small heels clacking loudly on the mirrored floor.

'Sponge your dress with this.' He handed her a spotless white hand towel and continued to rub at his suit.

'Thank you.' Jeannie turned on the ornate gold tap and dabbed in an embarrassed way at her skirt. She found the intimacy of the situation was making her heart pound unnaturally.

'Hmmm, make sure you soak it later. What was all the rush for? Were you late for an assignation?'

Jeannie's eyes flashed angrily. 'Of course not. I just had a good piece of news to tell Ben.'

One of Saif's eyebrows arched sardonically. 'I see. Personal news, or business?'

'Business,' she said stiffly.

'I'm glad to hear it. I hate my employees courting in my time.'

Jeannie gasped at his rudeness.

'Well,' he continued briskly, 'what is the news?'

'It's the site for the school in Safiq. I've got an ideal building—well within the budget. Here's a few plans I've sketched out. We could authorise work on it in a couple of weeks.'

Her enthusiasm had won over her annoyance with him. It really was a coup. She held out the plans proudly.

Saif took the sheaf of papers and his brows met in a frown when he saw the location.

'In here,' he said abruptly, walking to his desk.

His face retained its look of disapproval and Jeannie prepared herself for a scathing attack while Saif ran expert eyes over the drawings and began to check through her costings.

'Why don't you tell me it's a bad idea without keeping me in suspense?' she asked quietly.

'Bad?' Saif shook his head. 'For once, you underestimate yourself. I don't know how you've done it. Khaled has agreed to sell? You arranged all this?' His finger jabbed at the site map.

When she nodded, he shook his head in disbelief. 'Miss Bennett, I'm amazed. I've been after that site for months. It's perfect. I can see why you were pleased. Just explain these figures to me again.'

Hardly able to believe her ears, Jeannie stood by Saif's side and found the break-down of the totals.

'Hmm. I suggest you don't use Fasad for the clearance. He'll only contract it out and won't keep an eye on it. Try al Atrash. Excuse me . . .' He reached across Jeannie to his In tray and passed a file to her. 'Apart from that, you seem to have organised everything very well. Any problem with drainage?'

'None at all. Look . . .'

She thumbed through the papers. Saif's head bent closer to hers and she caught the now familiar faint fragrance of lime. Her body quivered but he seemed totally unmoved by her presence.

'Excellent, excellent. I like the layout. Make sure you keep me informed of the site progress.'

He slid into the huge leather chair at his desk, much to Jeannie's relief, examining the drawings anew. His delight and eagerness were catching.

'I could give you a weekly bulletin, if you like. I'm glad you approve,' she said.

Disarmingly, Saif swung round in his chair and faced her, smiling broadly.

'I approve, Miss Bennett, I approve of it all. I'm very impressed.'

There was that lurch inside her again. He could really turn on the charm when he wanted!

'Now,' he continued, 'can you cope with all this on your own?'

Jeannie nodded, eyes shining. His praise was rare enough to overwhelm her. She was aware that this would all mean a huge work-load, though. She hoped she was winning him over and showing him that not all Englishwomen were unreliable.

The warmth between them continued over the next few days. Several times they both became so involved in discussing plans that Jeannie became concerned at the bond which was growing between them. Saif's mind was quick to see the answers to problems on the site and Jeannie was full of admiration for the way he handled his employees. If only he wasn't such a bully out of working hours!

Rarely was she out of the building now before ten.

Whenever she left, however, the light still burned in Saif's office. If she was working flat out, then he was putting in even more hours. Not much of a family life for him. His women friends must be getting a raw deal, too!

Gradually, however, whenever their paths crossed, Jeannie noticed a strange light appearing in his eyes. It was as if he was watching her, judging in some way. He became critical, less relaxed, picking faults in her work quite unreasonably. It seemed he was trying to rattle her confidence. It became an effort to fulfil her duties and keep one step ahead of him.

After one particularly sharp exchange between them, there came a summons to his office. She'd dreaded this moment. Had she gone too far in stating her case? Hastily assembling all her arguments again before she confronted him, she walked slowly into Saif's office.

He raised his eyes briefly. 'Morning. Sit down.'

The Minister sat behind his huge desk. Ben was on the edge of a chair, looking very formal and on his guard.

'I hope you will forgive an immediate start on the matter for which I called you both here,' said Saif. 'It is urgent.'

CHAPTER FIVE

DRY-MOUTHED, Jeannie waited for the axe to fall. Saif looked particularly preoccupied and harassed. His tie had been loosened and his fingers were drumming an incessant rhythm on the desk. It was at that moment that Jeannie realised how much she enjoyed her job; how miserable she would be if Saif sacked her.

Her fears proved to be unfounded when the Minister began to speak.

'The Sultan is entertaining a dozen education experts from the British Department of Education. It was a sudden invitation, I believe—the Britons were as surprised as I was. They arrive in three weeks' time. Every school in Riyam is to be visited and the Sultan has asked that we make a special effort. I thought maybe an exhibition in the foyer here . . . However, I can't ask you to take on more work than you are doing already. I can only hope that you would be prepared to help somehow. Riyam must come out of this visit with honour. I'd hate the Sultan to be ashamed of the department.'

'No problem,' said Ben, exchanging glances with Jeannie. 'We can sort out a display.'

'Of course,' she cried warmly. 'I can organise each school, too. They could display the children's work. Then we can mount plans, drawings, statistics and other information in the foyer. Oh, and perhaps the Safiq children could do a short project on Riyam—writing, history, paintings and so on. That would look well with our official material.'

There was an admiring light in Saif's eyes at

Jeannie's unmistakable enthusiasm. 'I'm grateful for your support, thank you both,' he said quietly. 'Look, I think I'd better leave you alone for the next couple of weeks to keep other work to a minimum. I have to prepare information booklets for the visitors so that should keep me out of your hair. I appreciate your loyalty. Perhaps you'd better go now and discuss the details together.'

With a week to go, the exhibition was almost ready. Late one evening, Jeannie sprawled on the floor of the foyer, pasting pictures on to card, her mint-green skirt spreading in soft folds around her. Leaning forwards to reach for a fresh piece of card, she became aware of Saif's well-polished shoes a few inches from her hand. And she also became intensely aware of the view he must have of her breasts, partially exposed by her crisp open-necked white shirt. She sat up hastily.

'You make me feel like a slave-driver,' came his warm, husky voice.

'Well, I don't feel like a slave,' she replied briskly.

He crouched down very close to her, fixing her with those startlingly clear black eyes. 'I'm sure you don't,' he laughed.

Jeannie swallowed at the effect his nearness had on her. Damn! No doubt he was trying to disconcert her. Well, she wasn't going to give him the satisfaction of thinking that he affected her, whenever he turned on the charm. Even if she did want to reach up to him and put. . . . Oh, blast him! She was blushing!

'Miss Bennett.' How intimate he sounded, despite the formality of his words. 'I can't tell you how grateful I am for all the work you've done on this exhibition. It's an excellent display. Quite superb.'

'Oh, thank you. It was Ben as well.' His gratitude

was so sincere—and so unexpected—that she hardly
knew what to say.

'I know, and I've already expressed my thanks to
him. He said you had dealt with most of it. Miss
Bennett, I——' Saif raked his hands through his
hair, the dark curls immediately springing back on
to his forehead. Suddenly he seemed less intimidating, perhaps a little harassed and uncertain,
certainly more approachable. 'I made a mistake
about you when we ... uh ... first met. I want to
apologise for everything. It seems you do care, and
I'm full of admiration for the way you've worked.
I've made things difficult for you sometimes, I
know. Forgive me.' Saif's voice was low. 'There
were reasons why I was unwelcoming. Personal
reasons which shouldn't have intruded on my
judgment. I'm sorry.'

How could she resist those eyes, that tone! He was
infinitely seductive. He ought to have been an actor
with such a voice, thought Jeannie; he could have held
audiences spellbound. She struggled for composure
and said neutrally, 'I'd prefer to forget everything that
happened as well. But now you've brought up the
subject of our first meeting, perhaps you would clear
up one thing that's been puzzling me. Why did you
pretend your name was Tarik? Why did the driver call
you that?'

'I didn't pretend—it's my tribal name, the one used
by the Bedouin. Please don't remind me of my
behaviour that day; I'm ashamed of it, and would like
to make amends—to begin again. Perhaps we could
start our relationship off properly with a good dinner.'
He pulled her up, smiling disarmingly while keeping
hold of her hands. 'You can't work any more tonight;
it's past ten o'clock.'

As they had risen, close together, Jeannie had

recognized in him the signs of desire. Drat! Why did
he have to ruin it all?

'Oh, no, I couldn't possibly,' she said sharply.
Presumably he was hoping for a different kind of
relationship to begin. Dinner somewhere cosy, and
then back to the struggle in his arms. To hell with him
for his arrogant suppositions!

His hand pressed hers more firmly. 'Of course you
could. I'm only inviting you to dinner, not my bed,
Miss Bennett. You won't be compromised if you
accept.'

Jeannie flushed angrily, the friendly feelings
towards him fast disappearing in a great wave of
disappointment. 'I disagree. And you know it's not
proper for me to accept. You ought to be going home.
Isn't there someone waiting for you there?'

She purposely made her voice sound harsh. He
really didn't seem to have any morals at all, or any
thought for his wife. It was very late and he obviously
couldn't care less about rolling home in the small
hours.

'You talk like a governess. I'm a big boy—or haven't
you noticed? I stay out after ten quite often.' He
sounded amused. 'Mahine isn't waiting for me, if
that's what you're worried about. I rang her earlier
and told her I'd get something to eat. So she's not
expecting me back and we can go out for dinner after
all. Come on, I'm hungry.'

Jeannie couldn't believe how casual he was about his
wife. If this was a typical Arab marriage, she was sorry
for the women in this country. 'No, thank you. I have
no intention of spending the evening with you.'

Puzzled, he drew back. 'I promise I will treat you
with the utmost courtesy,' he said softly.

'You don't understand, do you—you're so bound up
in what you want, what you like to do, that you never

consider anyone else. Don't you think your Mahine
would like you home early for a change? Don't you
care about her?'

'Enough!' he cried. 'My feelings for Mahine are
none of your bloody business! You presume too much,
Miss Bennett. Remember you are an employee and
have no right to tell me what to do in my spare time.
What terrifies you about other people's kindness? I've
been very grateful for the work you've put in. I
wanted to say thank you by taking you to dinner.
Don't you know how rude it is to refuse a well-meant
gift? Why are you so disapproving? Why do you crush
any overtures I make? Are you afraid I might kiss you
again and perhaps release some of your undoubted
inhibitions about Arabs?' He pulled her close, his
chest rising and falling quickly.

To her horror, in full view of anyone who might be
walking past the glass entrance hall, he bent his head
low and kissed her deeply.

'I've been wanting to do that for a long time,' he
murmured. His mouth moved slowly over hers,
softening her angry lips till they plumped, full and
curving, into his. 'So beautiful. I've tried not to get
involved with you Jeannie, I swear it. If you won't
have dinner with me, will you come for a walk on the
beach—or perhaps you'd prefer a quiet drink in my
office?'

'Oh, no!' she cried, twisting in his grasp. 'I'm not interested in your propostions.'

'Really?' he breathed, pinning her more tightly.
'Your mouth says otherwise.'

He was right; she wanted him to go on and on. His
lips and tongue fired her brain till she couldn't think
straight; all she was conscious of was his hard,
demanding body and his hungrily roaming hands,
taking every liberty he wanted.

'I'm not giving in, I'm not!' thought Jeannie. Deliberately she let her body go rigid and her mouth hard.

'That's not very friendly,' Saif said in a coaxing voice.

'It's not supposed to be,' she said icily. 'Take your passions elsewhere. You've misjudged your appeal. You're not the kind of man I'm interested in.'

Swearing under his breath, he released her with a sigh. 'Still fighting your nature. I must be losing my touch.' He grinned ruefully. 'One day you'll realise what you want, but don't make me wait too long. I'm not used to being denied anything. I'd better leave you to your virgin bed, Miss Bennett. Here.' He thrust some keys into her hand. 'Lock up. I'm going to eat.'

Once again, he'd been able to do whatever he liked with her; taking her by surprise and daring to slip past her barriers without any qualm. He was the most unconventional, bombastic, arrogant man she'd ever known! He also kissed like a dream. She was still tingling from the sensation as Saif pushed his way through the swing doors without a backward glance. Despite all her resolutions, her reactions had been even worse than before. Softened by his charm and approval this time, she'd been close to putting her arms around him and letting the tide of his kisses sweep her along.

If they hadn't been in full view of the public; if they hadn't been talking about his wife a few moments before, she didn't know what she would have allowed. It was all so unfair! She must be starved of affection to behave like this.

It was time she became involved with the other men in the community. She was becoming neurotic about Saif. He was plainly not available yet for some reason he obsessed her, and he probably knew it. If she went out with someone else on a regular basis, maybe he'd leave her alone and she'd get some peace. She'd accept the next invitation that came her way.

But Saif wasn't so easy to forget. The dates she had merely emphasised his qualities, his good looks, of course—no one could compare with his strong dark face and burning eyes, nor his powerful physique; his air of authority; his sensual voice; his vigour. Within him she'd sensed a controlled energy that made him seem more alive, more vital, than anyone she'd ever met. And somewhere inside, she instinctively knew, was a tender and lonely man; locked, no doubt, in some arranged marriage that had never developed into a love-match. Poor Mahine! Saif probably drove her to distraction with his unfaithfulness.

Miserably Jeannie flopped on to the bed in her flat after another vaguely pleasant evening with one of the police officers. This wasn't helping! Her common sense told her that she was looking at Saif through rose-coloured spectacles, the men she went out with were surely far nicer, far more caring and attentive and most definitely unattached. Why, then did she brush aside all their good points and keep thinking of Saif?

With a deep sigh, she undressed and slipped into bed. The silk sheets caressed her body and she gave a little groan. She was stupidly fascinated by a married man. Whatever happened, she must keep the truth of her feelings from him because if he ever realised them, he'd have no compunction in seducing her.

Jeannie held her pillow tightly. If he tried, and the moment was right—somewhere private, with soft music, wine—she didn't know if she could stop herself from giving in. Then she'd have to live with herself afterwards and the awful knowledge that he was returning to his wife—and his wife's bed.

She slept badly that night. But in the morning, she'd steeled herself to the inevitable: she'd do her job as well as she could and live the same unemotional, unturbulent life she'd led before. No one, just no one, was going to penetrate her defences. Not even this black-eyed, black-haired devil!

It was not too difficult for Jeannie to avoid the Minister for a while. He was very preoccupied with the visiting team of experts, and she was only once drawn into the arrangements for the visit. With fifteen other men in the room, she felt safe and able to fulfil her duties confidently.

The visit went well and the schools programme was stepped up as a result. She and Ben had to attend the official opening ceremony for the Nafud school and were to travel with the Minister. Then, to her consternation, Ben had to drop out at the last minute to deal with a problem. It was with some trepidation that Jeannie walked to the Ministry alone. A whole day with Saif would be quite a challenge to her strength of mind.

His Mercedes was waiting outside. As she drew near, the driver's window slid down smoothly. 'If you're ready, we'll leave,' a familiar voice told her.

Jeannie stared. Saif was in the driving seat. Damn, no official driver! That meant they'd be alone for the whole journey. But she'd have to put up with it. 'I'm ready.'

The passenger door swung open and Jeannie hesitated.

'Something wrong?'

She supposed she couldn't sit in the back as if he was the chauffeur. The idea made her giggle as she slipped into the deep, comfortable leather passenger seat beside him.

With a curious glance at her, he reached into the

glove compartment and brought out a map. 'Before we start, let me show you the route, just in case you have any queries.'

Jeannie glanced at his wickedly gleaming eyes. Surely he couldn't be gently teasing her! What an extraordinary man.

'Now, I can't drive direct to Nafud, the roads are unsuitable for this car. I'm going north, then striking up this wadi. Does that meet with your approval?'

'It does and I'm glad you explained. I would have been looking out for the position of the sun.'

His answering grin stunned her with its openness. Thank heavens he was in a good mood. Jeannie relaxed as they drove off. Saif was showing an unexpected sense of humour!

'Perhaps we could call a truce for today, Miss Bennett? I've been working hard and am very tired. I don't have the energy to fight you continually. We'll be together till sunset and I'd prefer not to spend the next twelve hours scoring points against you,' he told her smoothly.

'That's all right by me.' She couldn't resist rising to his arrogance, however. 'But what makes you think *you'd* be scoring the points?'

Saif chuckled. 'I asked for that. Habits are difficult to break. I must try harder.'

'Yes, you really must,' thought Jeannie. He kept shooting glances at her as he negotiated a way through the city. His eyes strayed to her mint-green skirt. It had ridden up slightly and she was aware of his frank appraisal of her legs. The last time she had worn this outfit had been when he had asked her to dinner that night. Twelve hours alone together! She hoped she'd still be in one piece by the end of them. She didn't trust him one bit. Wriggling a little, she pulled ineffectually at her hemline, then rubbed damp palms on her legs. It was hot already, or was the heat from inside her?

'Sorry it's so hot in here. Once we get out of these narrow streets and can go faster, the air conditioning will work.'

He didn't miss a thing. She'd better keep the conversation on official lines and get his mind off her and her body. Jeannie was searching for an opening to start discussing the education system when a hard, tensed arm shot out across her chest and the car screeched to a halt. The next moment, Saif's anxious face was looming over hers, his body twisted around, his hands gently holding her shoulders.

'Are you all right?' he asked. He almost sounded concerned, she thought.

'I think so.' But there was a dull ache in her chest. 'My ribs hurt a bit.'

'I'm sorry. I had to stop you from shooting through the window. How's your neck?'

'My neck? Seems all right. What happened?'

'Thank Allah.' His relief astonished Jeannie. He was probably worried about his insurance or something. 'Wait here,' he commanded.

She leaned back and rubbed her chest. Saif's arm had felt like a steel bar against it. There'd been a momentary impression of his clenched fist and iron-hard muscles under the dark suiting, then her eyes had lifted in shock to see a small figure in the path of the car.

Had they run someone over? Unsteadily, she scrambled out. Saif was crouching down, talking quietly to a sulky young boy of about eight years old who was shielding a younger child. Both were ragamuffins, painfully thin and dirty, both clearly terrified. But Saif's coaxing voice eased their fears and soon they began to answer him shyly. Instinctively, Jeannie knew she mustn't intrude; whatever was happening, Saif was handling the situation very well. She watched the boys' timidity slowly change to willing enthusiasm. There was no doubt that Saif was a charmer; even just watching him she felt drawn by his warmth and sincerity.

Jeannie sighed. He really was very complex. A few weeks ago she wouldn't have believed that people could have so many sides to their character. Now she did. Even she seemed to be made up of more layers than she knew—after all, the old Jeannie would certainly have had difficulty in imagining herself in Tarik/Saif's arms.

The memory stirred her. She sat tensely as Saif straightened up, holding the children's hands, biting his lip when he saw her so watchful, so serious.

'You're not going to believe this, Miss Bennett,' he coughed in an embarrassed way, 'but I have to make a small detour. It's these boys, they need shelter. Only a short distance across the city, I assure you.'

'Of course.' Bewildered, Jeannie slipped back into the car while the boys tumbled excitedly into the back seat, jumping up and down on the smart upholstery.

'Just down here.'

'What happened? Are they all right?'

'Oh, yes. The younger one tripped and I nearly ran him over.' He seemed reluctant to say more and spoke pointedly to the chattering boys.

At a large white building, Saif and the boys clambered out and disappeared through an arched doorway. It was some time before Saif came out alone, looking very worried and thoughtful. He said nothing.

Naturally Jeannie was intensely curious, but for once she didn't pester him with questions immediately. When they had left Safiq and headed north, Saif's hands began to relax on the steering wheel and his shoulders lost their tense rigidity.

'Those children,' she began. 'Were they orphans, then?'

Saif nodded silently.

'That building was a children's home?'

'Yes.' He seemed very intent on the route suddenly.

'Why hadn't the boys gone there themselves?'

'It was full. No room.'

'You got them in.'

'I own it.' He smiled wryly. 'So the management didn't have much choice. But I've made it difficult for them. I've no idea how they'll cope—they're sleeping two to a bed already and the floors are covered with mattresses.'

'Isn't there anywhere else they can go?' She seemed to be asking an awful lot of questions.

'I'm building a larger home a few miles away, but it won't be ready for a few months.'

'You're very generous,' said Jeannie softly.

'No, I just know what it's like to be homeless. I'd do anything to keep the children off the streets.'

'I really can't see you as a scruffy, hungry little boy,' she said.

'Well, I was. And flea-ridden. And lousy. No child should have to beg for food, to fight for fish-heads on the quay, to search the dustbins in the barracks for anything edible.' His voice had become very quiet, as though he was talking to himself.

'God, how awful.' There was deep sympathy in her voice.

'I missed my father desperately when he died. He was so gentle, you see . . .' Emotion made him stop.

'My father meant a lot to me, too,' she ventured. 'We were inseparable. He was a writer and manoeuvred his hours so that he had time for me after school. Looking back on it now, I should imagine my mother was a bit put out at the hours we spent together.'

'So, we have something in common. And, it seems, you are a sensitive woman after all. You feel passionately.'

'No!' Jeannie was shocked. The two feelings didn't go together at all.

'Hmm, you don't understand yourself. Only a deeply passionate woman would be so affected by the loss of her father.'

'I idolised him. He was so . . . caring.'

'Another man will take his place one day. One who will care for you also.'

'I doubt it. I don't find men very appealing.' Excluding him, of course, she mused.

'You will. Everyone needs someone to love. Even Ministers of Education.' Saif grinned ruefully.

She longed to reach out and touch him. 'But you're successful. You've come a long way.'

'Not really. I have money and power but I'm still alone.'

The intimacy of his words hung in the air. Cocooned together in the enclosed space of a twentieth-century creation, passing through the timeless desert landscape, Jeannie recognised his unspoken need to talk and his unconscious need for comfort.

'People think a lot of you,' she said warmly. 'You're held in great affection.'

'I know. However, it's hardly the same as having someone of your own.'

'No, it's not,' thought Jeannie wistfully. 'But he has got a family, unlike me.'

'Your home,' she began.

'I prefer to work.'

How bitter his voice sounded! 'That can't be enough, surely?'

'No, it's not. I'm just discovering that.'

For a while he was silent, as if fighting an urge to

confide further. Jeannie was upset by his rejection of his wife and children.

'Miss Bennett, forgive me—I've talked more than I intended. I'm not quite sure why. You have a quality . . . Please forget what I've said.'

'I can keep confidences. I'm not the gossiping sort.'

'No, I don't think you are. Thank you. Now, I think we should go over the day's events.'

The next few hours passed more pleasantly than Jeannie could have imagined. Those shared moments had added something to their relationship. Saif was an agreeable and interesting companion, full of fascinating information about the area and its people. He related stories with that special warmth of his, sprinkling them with amusing anecdotes that betrayed a dry sense of humour.

A ring of forts, each with fascinating histories, lined the approach to the foothills and Nafud. There was the Tower of the Birds, a look-out for slavers who rang its bell when the Sultan's soldiers approached so that the citizens of Nafud could hustle their slaves into tunnels below the city. There were the fields of lucerne and indigo, spreading cool green, restful to the eyes after the baking desert.

Acres of palms filled the horzion. Nafud sprawled across the valley and slopes of a hill at the meeting of three wadis. It was a secret and holy city, its massive fort dominating the plain. Saif told her how a few men had lain under siege in the fort for nearly four years until one of the men heard his wife was pregnant and left the gate open as he slipped out to see her. It was only after the fort was taken that the man realised that a nine-month pregnancy didn't match up with his four-year absence.

Their shared laughter at the ancient legend made Jeannie worry about the sensation of ease between them. She almost willed him to be cruel to her again; this delight in his company was more than she could handle. Every moment he unwound a little more, acted more naturally with her and showed her his pleasant side. It made rejection more difficult.

He opened the little school with dignity, deferring to the officials and flattering the elders. After ceremonial coffee, he insisted on joining the children and sat under a lemon tree with them, telling stories that made them alternatively squeal with laughter or open their eyes wide in excitement. Eventually, he removed his jacket, undid his heavy gold cuff links and rolled up his sleeves to play a wild game of basketball. Jeannie hesitated; it looked such fun. On impulse, she slipped off her shoes and reached out to catch the ball just as it soared past. For a moment there was a shocked silence, then cries of glee.

'If you're playing on the girls' side, then I'm playing for the boys,' she called to Saif.

'Right, Miss Bennett. No holds barred,' he retorted, grinning.

Jeannie was sorry when they had to leave. The children and their families stood with the dignitaries and roared their approval as the Mercedes drew away.

'Whew, I'm exhausted!' Without thinking, she pulled off the ribbon which tied back her hair and ran her fingers through the unruly waves.

'I'm not surprised. Ever played for the Harlem Globetrotters?'

'No!' she laughed. 'My legs were too short.'

His roar of laughter startled her. 'I've no complaints about your legs, Miss Bennett. You need cooling down, though, and it's too hot to travel. We'll have our late lunch now.'

The small oasis where they stopped was quite beautiful. Tucked in a hollow carpeted with tiny daisies, it supported an extraordinary variety of fruit trees. Saif pointed to a scrubby-looking bush.

'That's a frankincense tree,' he said.

'But it's ugly!' exclaimed Jeannie.

'Yet it gives one of the most rare and enticing perfumes. Strange, isn't it? We're all ugly in one way or another, yet beautiful too. Don't you agree?'

She was too astonished to answer. She'd never realised he might think in this way.

They sat by a well and Saif brought a hamper from the car.

'There's enough for three here, of course. Pity Ben couldn't come. We might have won the game. Wine?'

'Er, yes, thank you.' She sipped the heady wine and broke off a piece of soft bread, lying in the shade and enjoying the chicken and fruit. In her nervousness, she drank more wine than she intended until, throwing back her head, she stretched luxuriously. 'I feel all muzzy,' she said faintly.

'Wine and heat don't mix. There's time for a sleep.'

Jeannie lay back, meaning only to rest for a few moments but was soon fast asleep with Saif watching over her. When she woke, he'd come closer and was covering her with his jacket. The sound of cicadas filled the air, lending an exotic quality to the night.

'I didn't mean to waken you,' he said softly.

'What . . .?'

'It's getting chilly.'

'And quite dark!' she exclaimed.

'You were tired. You expended a lot of energy today.'

'Not really—I drank too much wine. I'm sorry. I've made you very late.'

'No problem,' he said. 'I've nothing to get back for. And I don't want today to finish. It's been more fun than I expected.'

'You really love being with children, don't you?' asked Jeannie.

'The children? Oh, yes. They make simple demands that I can cope with.'

'Who doesn't make simple demands, then?'

'Women—especially British women.' Bitterness tinged his voice.

'All of them?'

'All the ones I've known—except you, maybe.'

'But you're not sure.'

'No, you puzzle me. You work like a man, sometimes speak like a man, but always you remain feminine.'

'Thank you! If that was a compliment.'

They grinned at each other, then looked seriously into each other's eyes. Saif placed his hands on either side of Jeannie as she lay propped up on one elbow, her soft golden hair falling over one eye. His strong body moved closer and she was trapped by the tender look on his face. No one had ever looked at her like that before.

'May I kiss you?' he asked huskily.

'I'm surprised you asked,' she defended herself, and could have bitten her tongue when she saw the hurt in his eyes. 'I'm sorry, you're muddling me. I'm confused.'

'So am I. You haven't answered my question.'

Jeannie swallowed. He seemed nervous and vulnerable. She'd seen such gentleness in him; it was poignant that such a caring man was wasted by being married to a woman he didn't love. But he was married, she mustn't forget that.

'It's not right,' she said. 'You're in no position to kiss me.'

'On the contrary, I'm in the perfect position. I have only to reach out and my lips would touch yours.'

Such logic! If only she didn't tremble so. 'Please don't spoil everything. I like you, I respect and admire you. Please don't make things difficult. We've got to work together, after all.'

'Will you let me kiss you, or not?' he persisted.

'Not.'

'For the love of Allah, why? What antique morals prevent it? Let down that barrier. It's not really you. Inside that reluctant woman is a creature of strong desires. I know you want me to kiss you. The fullness of your lips tells me that.' His own mouth was very close—too close.

Darn it, he could read her like a book. 'My standards aren't antique,' she said stiffly. 'Please move back and let me sit up. My arms ache.'

'So do mine.' He pushed her gently down on the ground, his breath whispering in her ear. 'You need courting? I'll court you. In a week or so there's a Consulate Ball. Come as my partner.'

Jeannie's green eyes clouded in disappointment at his tactlessness. 'How could I! That would outrage everyone there. How can you suggest such a thing? In everyone's eyes it would seem as if you were openly setting me up as your mistress!'

'What a good idea.'

The effrontery of the man! Jeannie's mouth opened in protest and was immediately covered by his demanding lips. She struggled furiously, trying to disentangle herself, wincing suddenly at a sharp pain in her neck. Saif jerked back immediately, full of concern.

'Oh, my neck!'

'You poor girl. That'll be from our sudden stop this morning. It often takes a few hours before a whiplash injury shows itself. I'm sorry. Here.'

He hauled himself behind her, so that Jeannie was

pulled against his chest. The pain was too sharp for her to bother about what he was doing but she was relieved to feel his long fingers deftly massaging the muscles in her neck, easing the tension considerably. After a while the sharp dagger-like pains shooting through her head had lessened, but still Saif continued, gently kneading and probing.

Jeannie felt very contented, relaxed into companionship. All she wanted was to stay there, safely encircled by his arms. The sandgrouse dipped to the water and she wished she was free like them, to live and . . . She dismissed the thought that sprang to her mind.

'Please don't let me be falling in love with him! Let it be the wine!' She tried to sit up.

'I think it's all right now.' She rolled her head to test it.

'Just relax for a moment.' He lifted her back again and folded his arms around her. With him she felt so secure, so happy and at peace.

'How light you are. Like a delicate flower,' he said softly. They both remembered the time the butterfly had alighted on her shoulder, and Jeannie blushed.

'A pink rose-bud, sweetly perfumed.'

As if to verify his words, a cool breeze sprang up, wafting the scent of lemon and frankincense towards them. The black sky blazed with thousands of brilliant lights, making Jeannie feel unimportant and puny. What did the past and the future matter when the present was so special?

Slowly, Saif turned her round, staring at her longingly. He reached out to take her hands in his and raised them to his lips, kissing each finger with infinite tenderness then running his lips to her wrist. Jeannie gave a sharp intake of breath. His eyes were drawn to the swelling breasts under the crisp shirt.

'We must go back.' She struggled with her desires, and the rights of his wife.

'Not yet. I want to stop time. To stay here and pretend nothing else exists.'

'You can't allow yourself to do that,' breathed Jeannie.

'I must! If there was no hope . . .' Wildly, he dragged her to him, running his lips over her face in a fury of kisses. His hands cautiously touched her shoulders as he feathered a light murmuring kiss on her lips. She couldn't, wouldn't stop him, but instead demanded him with her mouth, surrendering to the mounting tension in her body and the tight hardness of him against her thighs. His skin trembled at her touch on his back, then he groaned deeply and gently unbuttoned her shirt. Then, his teeth biting deep into his own lip in passion, he slid off her bra. She strained for the touch of his long fingers but he just held her, gazing in wonder at the erratic rise and fall of her breasts till she could bear it no more.

'Touch me, please!' she whispered. It was as if a thousand knives were stabbing flames through her body.

Like a man in a daze, Saif slowly raised his hands and cupped her breasts softly, cradling them in his smooth fingers, curving his hands around their full warmth as she breathed heavily at his touch. With unbelievable delicacy, he rubbed their dusky peaks till they rose, erect and hard, pulsing with the life he had given them. The sweet pain of desire thudded with an insistent throbbing that blotted out all thought, all knowledge of what she was doing or where she was. She slid her hands down his back to massage his skin in rhythm with his hands which were urging such unbelievable responses from her breasts. Quivering, he raked a questing mouth over her slim throat and the hollow between her breasts, then bent his handsome head and ran his tongue lightly over the surging centre of one rounded globe. A wild shudder thrilled throughout her body, setting every nerve aflame; echoed by ripple after ripple of pleasure as he closed his lips on her nipple, licking and nibbling and setting up a terrible emptiness in her body.

'I want you,' he murmured. 'Here, now.'

On the brink of relinquishing herself completely, she drew back. 'Not that,' she whispered. 'Not that.'

'You can't deny me now.'

'I can—I will.' Jeannie struggled awkwardly to sit up, hampered by his stroking hands.

'Why are you so afraid of me? Or is it just sex that terrifies you?'

Jeanne swallowed hard and lowered her eyes. 'I don't want to get involved. I need to concentrate on my job. Men would complicate my life. Please don't do that!' The soft folds of her skirt were being gently pushed further up her legs. 'I'm a career girl. I . . .'

'Look at me. Be honest for once.' His hands felt so smooth on her thighs.

'Oh!' She threw back her head in an unconsciously seductive gesture of abandon. As Saif bent, his mouth moistening her nipple, she shuddered and pushed against him.

'Damn you, you've got me drunk! There's no other way you could have done this.' She refused to admit how she felt. Her reactions had totally unnerved her. What could she say to put him off? 'I will admit, Minister, you're quite good. It was nice. That's as far as it goes, though. You really ought to realise that you're totally unsuitable for me.'

'Nice! Tell me, then, who *is* suitable?' His low voice had a dangerous quality to it now.

Jeannie winced. Her words had certainly stopped him in his tracks. If only she could keep going, she'd save her reputation. 'Well,' she said casually, 'Englishmen are suitable, of course.'

'Any Englishman?'

'More or less.'

'Like those men you've been going out with?'

'You've been spying on me!'

'Not much goes on in Safiq without my knowing. People tell me things.'

'Yes,' she thought. 'I'm getting rid of Nava right away.'

'I've had fun,' she lied. 'They're very amusing.'

'I thought you had better taste.' There was agony on his face. 'You disappoint me, Miss Bennett.'

'I'll bet I do,' she replied, hardly able to bear the hurt she had caused him. 'Take me back to Safiq now. It's been a very pleasant day.'

His breath hissed painfully but he obeyed. She wondered if she'd gone too far. They didn't speak after that. Several times, Jeannie wanted to reach over and touch Saif's sad face. She'd hurt his pride and touched a raw nerve, but her words had hurt her as much as they had hurt him.

'I didn't mean it!' she cried to herself. 'I didn't mean to hurt you!'

For it seemed unbelievably cruel of her. Today, with the orphans, he'd exposed his inner self— probably for the first time. She'd been placed in a position of trust. Now she had thrown that back in his face. The incident with the boys showed a tender, caring nature. Why had he wanted to confide in her? Ah well, perhaps if she removed herself from the scene, he might begin to open up to his wife. While Saif hoped that Jeannie might respond to him, he was preventing the proper growth of his relationships at home.

'All very rational and objective,' thought Jeannie

bitterly. 'But I want him to make love to me. I want to talk to him! I want him to tell me all about himself. Why can't I turn back the clock and have no feelings again? I knew all this emotion was a mistake! How on earth am I going to last the next two months?'

She had no contact with the Minister for some time afterwards, not even a memo. He came and went well outside everyone else's working hours, and instead of wandering casually into offices to speak to people, he summoned them to him. The atmosphere in the building was one of gloom, since Saif's depression and irritability affected everyone employed by him.

Hearing that he'd planned to meet his brother and leave early one night, Jeannie felt safe enough to work late. Dreading confrontation, she had no intention of chancing a hostile scene with him—it upset her too much. Maybe if she worked hard tonight she could clear up some of the routine paperwork on her desk and fit in a couple more school visits. It was important that she had all the ends of her job tied up by the end of the three months. Then she could decide whether to stay or not.

At nine o'clock she stretched her aching back and reached for the coffee pot. Darn! It was empty. The nearest source was the Minister's office. She was certain he'd gone. Any signs of a light under his door and she'd have to raid one of the other offices instead.

The outer office was in darkness, but the moon shone brightly through the window. His office was empty. Jeannie stood silently for a moment, remembering the first time she'd entered it: she had been so eager and hopeful then. Chiding herself for useless reverie, she went to a sandalwood cupboard which glowed silver in the moonlight. Lifting the pot of coffee, she knocked it carelessly against a cut glass decanter.

'You could make me a cup, too.'

Jeannie swung round guiltily at the sound of his voice. 'What are you doing here?' she cried.

Saif grinned suddenly, his teeth flashing white in the dark shadows. He clicked the light on, looked her up and down, then switched it off again. 'No, Miss Bennet, I should say that. This is my office, remember?' He sat down in an easy chair, sounding vastly amused.

'I was working and I ran out of coffee. What were you doing in the dark?' she accused.

'Come and see.'

It might be unwise to obey, but she was curious. From his chair Saif had a view over the harbour. 'I like moonlight. It's very calming. See——' he caught her hand and drew her down to his level '——the moon lights the whole bay and turns the sea to melting silver. How lovely it all is.'

He began to speak the lines of a poem, so softly that Jeannie had to strain to hear the words.

> *The night has a thousand eyes*
> *And the day but one,*
> *Yet the light of the bright world dies*
> *With the dying sun.*
>
> *The mind has a thousand eyes,*
> *And the heart but one;*
> *Yet the light of a whole life dies*
> *When love is done.'*

There was a catch in his voice, and conflicting emotions swept visibly across his expressive face. He must have thought he was in darkness, but Jeannie could see that his eyes were moist.

'That's lovely,' she said quietly.

When he turned to her, still holding her hand, she started at the sadness in his face. 'At the end of the day, before I go home, I watch the stars come out. My life pales into insignificance beside that sky. And I wonder if it matters whether I keep on fighting my instincts. Who would care if I lived as my body tells me?'

'I would have thought you did that already.'

Gently, Saif smiled at her. 'If only you knew. Most of the time I'm under tight control. You'd be surprised at what I'm really like.'

'So would your wife,' thought Jeannie.

She stood up abruptly. 'I'll make the coffee.' The silence between them became uneasy.

'Why did you tell Nava to leave?' he asked suddenly.

'I didn't need her.'

'I thought she was useful. Everyone needs someone to talk to. I need someone tonight. Once I confided in you. Can I do so again?' he asked.

'You could go home.'

'Please don't start that. It's more peaceful here. I've had a hard day and I need civilised company. Stay for a moment at least.' He sounded so wistful that Jeannie relented. She owed him some courtesy after treating him so badly. She sat on the floor, unsettled by his gentle voice, unwilling to walk out on him.

Once again she felt that peace, that companionship stealing over them. They sat in easy silence, the silver light gleaming around them.

'I could stay with him here forever,' Jeannie mused. 'Just sitting with him. Oh, hell! I thought I had problems when I just wanted him. Now I'm definitely close to falling in love. With Saif I'd be content, whatever we were doing. Just sitting is enough.'

She became aware that she was being studied carefully.

'I've been thinking a lot about you, Miss Bennett.'

She should never have accepted his invitation to sit down. It must have given him ideas.

'Are you going to stay?' he continued.

'Only a moment.'

'No, I meant after the three months.'

'Oh, I don't know. I'm not sure.'

'I think you should. I'm being very selfish in saying so, of course, though I think such a decision would be to your benefit as well.'

'Really?' Jeannie's tone was non-committal.

'Yes. I very much want you to stay. You're a very good assistant. You're enthusiastic and loyal, imaginative and courteous. This is more than a job to you; you care. I want people like that in this department. We need people like you. Don't let us down by leaving.'

'If I leave, it won't be because of the job,' she said. Would he realise what she was talking about?

'You like the job?'

'It's a challenge, it's exciting. The best job I've ever had.' 'Or am ever likely to have,' she thought.

'Then you'll stay!' His face broke into an expression of pure delight, astonishing her. For a long time he held her gaze and her eyes automatically responded to his, softening and widening. He reached out and touched her shoulder. 'Just give it time. Accept your nature,' he said.

She didn't understand but before she could reply, he let his hands drop.

'It's time we both went home.'

A harsh voice came from the doorway: 'It certainly is.'

'Ahmed!' Saif exclaimed.

CHAPTER SIX

SAIF'S brother was gripping the doorframe, a grim shadowy copy of his brother.

'Sorry to break up your ... work,' he said sarcastically. 'You said you'd pick me up at this time.'

With a quick irritated glance at his watch, Saif stood up and shrugged his shoulders.

'You're right. I'm late. I lost track of the time.'

'I'll bet you did!'

'Ahmed!'

'Thank you for the coffee, Minister,' interrupted Jeannie, loath to be involved in this exchange. 'I'll be leaving now if you want to lock up.'

'I'll run you back.' Saif pushed some papers into his briefcase.

'No, thank you. I want to walk.' She had no intention of sharing a car with Ahmed. She could smell the drink from here.

When they reached the entrance hall, she realised that in her haste to get away she had left her bag in her office. Saif and Ahmed waited for her to retrieve it, intending to see her off the premises, but they had fallen into a fierce argument by the time Jeannie stepped out of the lift.

If she had only ignored their quarrel and swept out past them, she could have avoided the embarrassment of eavesdropping, but she hesitated in the darkened hall, watching their angry silhouettes against the huge glass doors.

'And you're a fool!' Ahmed was saying. 'You'll never learn.'

'Keep out of my life!' hissed Saif.

'Listen, she's just playing you along, as they all do. Don't you know that? She's after your money, just like Kate was after mine.'

'Shut up, Ahmed,' growled Saif.

'You won't hear anything against her, will you? She's tough. She'll hobble you like a camel. Grasping tarts, they are, women of her race. You ought to know that. Don't you remember what misery our dear mother caused?'

'That's enough!'

Ahmed's voice was growing hysterical. 'If you repeat the mistakes made by father and me, you're a fool. This woman is wrong for you.'

'Calm down.' Saif put an arm around his brother's shoulder only to be pushed away savagely.

'Don't touch me—you've been touching her! Go on, then, play her game and see how much it hurts when you find out how little she cares. And stay away from me and Mahine.'

'Leave Mahine out of it,' warned Saif.

'No. She has as much of a hang-up about the English as we do. It's not been easy for her, knowing you're running around with that blonde. She has feelings, after all.'

Ahmed staggered against the door as if to leave.

'Come here!' Saif lunged after his brother, catching his jacket. They both tumbled against the wall of the building, struggling together for a moment before Saif pinioned Ahmed against the door.

Jeannie felt awful. Not only had she come between husband and wife, but the two brothers as well. Ahmed seemed so distressed. That lovely moment with Saif had been destroyed by all this bitterness. It was up to her to let Ahmed know she didn't intend to pursue Saif.

'Sorry to be so long,' she said brightly, stepping

forward. 'I wonder if you can give me a lift, after all? I think I'll go to a friend's house tonight.'

The two men exchanged glances. 'A friend?' queried Saif tightly. 'Who? I mean, where do I drop you?'

'A police-officer friend. He lives on the police estate. You know it?'

'Get in.'

Jeannie trembled inwardly at the look on Saif's face. 'I . . . er . . . I might be a little late in the morning,' she said, her heart thumping with the lie. 'I'm not sure whether my friend can give me a lift in to work or not.'

No one answered her but Saif jammed his foot viciously on the accelerator till, with a screech of brakes, he drew up at the apartments indicated by Jeannie. She pretended to fumble for a key and the Mercedes drove off in a wild flurry of dust. Jeanie leant against the wall, tired out. Now she had to slog all the way back home. What a mess she had landed herself in!

If only Saif wasn't married. He had come to mean so much in her life and she hated him to think so badly of her. When she had slid out of the car, his face showed the contempt he felt for her promiscuity. One day she would like him to find out for himself that no man had made love to her. She reddened at the thought and sighed at its impossibility. It was important that he did think badly of her, however much she disliked the idea.

As she walked slowly home, her mind worked on ways to put him off her. He seemed too obsessed with her to take 'no' for an answer. Still, his pride was obviously shaken when she pretended to prefer other men; maybe she could develop that line a little.

Having an employer trying to seduce you was a difficult enough situation. When part of you wanted him to succeed, even knowing about his family ties, it was terrible. Someone had once told Jeannie that it was just as adulterous to wish or imagine an affair with a married man as it was actually to carry it out.

All her upbringing reviled the weakness of women who destroyed marriages. Yet she wanted Saif. How could she betray her strict code of behaviour like this? It wasn't love, it wasn't! It was just something unpleasant; a hidden lustful side of her that must be subdued.

She put to the back of her mind the rapport she had felt with Saif when they had worked on projects; the pleasure she had known when he praised her, and the warmth they had shared in those special quiet moments. But the insidious knowledge of their strange compatibility refused to be banished. There was something rare about their relationship. She couldn't have imagined it.

On the day before the Consulate Ball, Ben rang through to her office in a panic. 'Jeannie! Are you busy at four o'clock? Is it anything you can get out of? I need a favour.'

'Go on, what is it?' she asked indulgently.

'I've got to go to Nafud—there's an awful fuss brewing. Trouble is, I've promised them at Bij that I'd go to their school party. Can you do the Bij trip instead of me?'

'Help! What would I have to do?'

'Nothing! Just be there. They've decided to celebrate the first anniversary of the school. I'll ring up and explain. They're very nice people. Only two teachers, both Riyami, both bilingual. It's just a party for the kids, Jeannie.'

'I'll go. Just let me know how to get there.'

She was quite relieved to be busy. As the night of the ball had come closer, she had wavered about her decision to wear an exotic green dress that she had brought. If she did wear it, she knew the kind of reaction it would get. It would take quite a lot of nerve to carry it off.

The little school was right on the beach at Bij, serving the small fishing community. Jeannie could hear the sounds of a party in full swing long before she stepped through the low door of the schoolroom.

All the desks had been ranged along the walls to form a continuous table for the huge dishes of food and carafes of iced sherbet. The two teachers were just ushering the children towards the spread when they noticed Jeannie.

'Welcome! Come in and join our party!' cried the woman. 'I am Ashti, this is Abdullah.'

Jeannie shook hands with the man, who smiled gently at her.

'We will eat first, then play games on the beach,' he said, handing her a plate.

Within a short time, Jeannie was totally involved. The children were very natural and forthcoming, making it easy for her to talk to them in halting Arabic. Some of them taught her new words, squealing with laughter at her pronunciation.

Then Jeannie saw Ashti carrying in a young girl, aged about seven. 'Can you help Stela?' asked Ashti. 'She cannot walk or move her body—only her head and arms. Please take the food to her.'

'Of course,' replied Jeannie warmly. The little girl was lovely. She had long glossy black hair reaching to her waist and huge black eyes which sparkled in her tiny face. Stela had a small appetite and was soon satisfied with the few cakes on her plate, then she raised thin arms to Jeannie and gave her a hug.

All the other children screamed in delight at the sound of a car outside and rushed to the door. Stela wriggled in Jeannie's grasp as a man entered the schoolroom, totally swamped by children clinging to every part of him. With Stela's hair in her face, Jeannie couldn't see who it was at first.

He sank to the floor under the weight of the children's bodies and Jeannie caught a glimpse of a fine silver-grey suit before the crowd of children swarmed over him. They laughed and shouted in pleasure. The man was somewhere under a mass of bouncing bodies, making fierce growling noises. He rose, gently shrugging them off, arms extended, his face distorted into a wild snarl. The children scattered with joyful yells as he stalked stiff-legged towards them.

Jeannie had frozen. Not Saif! She wasn't mentally prepared for him. Especially with him acting like this. Stela gurgled with delight as he caught a handful of children and tumbled them to the floor, pretending to eat them. He then caught Ashti's eye and raised his head. 'Where's Stela?' he asked. Jeannie understood his Arabic and shrank against the wall. Stela yelled: 'I'm here!' and Saif looked in their direction.

His surprise was as great as Jeannie's. He stood in the middle of the milling children, stretching to full height and pushing back his tousled hair as they clamoured at his legs. With two boys hauling themselves up his body, he moved awkwardly over to Jeannie.

Tenderly he placed his arms around Stela and raised her high above his head, shaking her gently in the air as her pathetically thin legs dangled helplessly. Gently lowering her, he kissed her rosy cheeks as she wrapped her arms around his neck, raining kisses on his bronze face.

Jeannie felt a stab of pain run through her as he cradled the child in his arms and buried his head in her long glossy hair. Jeannie's heart lurched. His long lashes were moist. When he raised his face, it showed a strange and terrible agony and his eyes were shining with unshed tears.

Jeannie couldn't make him out at all. Unkind, unthinking to his family, using women for his pleasure, taking advantage of any willing woman—yet so emotional about deprived children. This visit hadn't been arranged to impress anyone. The children knew him; he'd obviously been before and played happily with them.

His jaw had tightened at Jeannie's assessing gaze. They were alone now, Ashti and Abdullah having ushered the children out to the beach.

'Where's Ben?' asked Saif, his voice shaking with emotion.

'In Nafud. A crisis.'

'You knew I'd be here?'

'No,' she said vehemently.

The silence between them was broken by Ashti collecting Stela. Saif spoke softly in rapid Arabic and Ashti left with the protesting child. With his toe, he kicked the door shut.

'What are you doing?' Jeannie felt nervous.

'We must have a talk. I last told you it would be unfortunate if you left. Now I've thought it over and I think it would be disastrous if you stayed.'

'So I'm no longer any good at my job?'

'I'm not talking about your job. I'm talking about the situation. I can't handle it. It's upsetting Ahmed too much—and me, of course.'

'What situation?' mumbled Jeannie.

'My feelings for you.'

The intimacy of his words, linking both of them together, nearly defeated her resolve. Then his remorseless gaze raked Jeannie's body with its customary arrogance. Immediately she felt her blood stir and her hackles rise. He had the power to anger and excite her. Just a look, a touch, and she seemed to melt before this man. Before he took advantage of this, she ought to attack.

'Your feelings are perfectly clear to me. Have you ever wondered, Minister, what *my* feelings are? At the risk of being sacked on the spot, I think I should tell you that I think you're a bastard. A shallow, pleasure-seeking bastard.'

He sucked in his breath. 'You don't think that at all. You have the same feelings as me. I can prove it.' He moved closer till she could smell the lime scent on his skin. She pressed back against the wall. His broad chest barred her escape and he placed his hands on the wall to either side of her, trapping her completely.

'Don't shame me any more!' she pleaded.

'Shame you?' he muttered through his teeth. 'I'm the one who's been shamed. All week you've invaded my thoughts, forced painful memories into my mind, ripped apart my sensible ordered life! At night I've imagined you in the arms of other men: unworthy men. You give yourself too cheaply; you're worth more than you give yourself credit for. And yet I still want you. Despite the fact that you sleep with half-grown policemen, I desire you.

'I have to know, Miss Bennett, what it is about you that threatens my comfortable existence and puts my life at home in danger. I have to get you out of my system once and for all. You have no real reason to refuse me: in the dark you wouldn't find me very different from any of the other men you patronise. So I will not accept any more refusals. I need to stop thinking about you. I must stop you becoming an obsession. This is the only way I know how.'

'Oh no!' whispered Jeannie as his head bent closer and his intentions became apparent. 'I don't want to interfere with your life.'

'The hell you don't. You've slipped like a viper into it.' He moved his hands down to her shoulders, gently circling his palms in slow rhythmic movements. 'I intend to take what's going and then wave you a final farewell at Safiq airport.'

'Everyone's waiting out there,' she breathed.

'Later. First, you.'

With infinite delicacy, he lifted his fingers to her throat, his light touch sending tingles vibrating through her body. He tenderly cupped her chin with one hand, caressing the nape of her neck with the other and releasing the demurely tied hair. He tangled both hands in her curls. Jeannie shut her eyes, unable to resist the promise of his movements, incapable of preventing him from touching her as he pleased. Her lips parted and she heard him give a deep, pain-ridden sigh.

He held her head between his palms, forcing her to look at him. She shuddered at the intensity in his dark, glowing eyes. As his lips moved imperceptibly towards hers, she was consumed by a devouring fire. Her lips pouted to meet his; her jade-green eyes clouded with desire.

'My sweet,' he murmured. 'Sweet Jeannie. Beautiful flower,' he murmured, his lips nearly touching hers. 'Are you a passive flower? Or maybe a trap?'

The lines on his face tautened at these last words and he drew in his breath harshly before pressing a savage kiss upon her mouth that rocked her almost off her feet with its intensity. All sense of reality had disappeared; she was sinking beneath his onslaught, conscious only of the violence of his impassioned attack. Her arms crept around his neck and she stroked the black curls on his neck. He held her more tightly and murmured soft words into her lips, Arabic words that she didn't understand.

Gentle hands caressed her arms, running lightly down her bare skin and sending shivers of anticipation rippling through her body. Jeannie touched his angular cheekbones, feeling the smooth golden skin, and tracing her fingers over the outline of his sensuous mouth. He reached up and caught her hands in his, putting each finger to his mouth and gently, ardently, sucking its tip, his eyes fixed intently on hers as she quivered in delirious ecstasy.

Again his mouth sought hers, nibbling and sucking softly at the swell of her lower lip. Then his teeth were nipping at her throat and his hands were trying to unfasten the buttons of her dress. With an involuntary movement, she caught at his hands in an attempt to stop him, but he merely kissed her again until her arms wound around his neck and twisted in his hair wildly.

Darting his tongue between her parted lips with swift practised movements, he made her forget his intended invasion. Then he pressed one hand against her trembling breast, feeling its full roundness and resisting all her efforts to push him away. His fingers fumbled with her buttons and slipped inside to touch her warm skin. A tremor rippled through his body, finding its response in her own shudders of pleasure.

He leaned back slightly from her and she opened her eyes to his yearning face.

'Do you want me to stop?' he breathed.

She bit her lip and shook her head wordlessly, limp and without resistance.

'We must wait a little while, my beautiful flower. This is not the place. Soon, very soon, I will show you what lovemaking really is.' Reluctantly he drew back, and smoothed his hair. 'We must go to the children,' he said huskily.

Jeannie heard the passion in his voice as he fought for self-control.

'You are answering the questions I have struggled with over the past few days. I am beginning to know why you fill me with such impetuous fire. Don't look at me like that! For the love of Allah, can't you see I'm trying to compose myself?' He looked down at her rumpled dress. 'Tidy yourself up and come on to the beach. I told Ashti we had a problem to discuss in private. Don't make her think I've been ravishing you!'

With difficulty, Jeannie buttoned up her dress, steadying her nerves. It probably wouldn't do for Ashti to know that her god, Saif, was attempting to seduce one of his employees, she thought bitterly. Thank heavens he'd stopped. If he hadn't, she wouldn't have cared where they were or what he was doing. Now, at a little distance, she must pull herself together.

Steeling all her resolve, she reached out and touched his arm. The urgency of his response terrified her as he whirled round, pulling her against him, kissing her neck wildly and bruising her mouth with his. He groaned with desire as Jeannie tore her lips from his.

'No!' she cried, pressing against the hard wall of his chest. 'That's not what I meant. I must talk to you—we must come to an understanding.'

He gazed down on her, smiling at her words. 'Yes, we must do that. I'll take you back to Safiq. We can talk then—your driver can go on his own. Now, come and join the children!' With a grin, he pushed the door open and stepped into the sunshine.

He had misunderstood. She wanted to tell him that however much they were attracted to each other, the relationship couldn't go anywhere. He was married and she was not prepared to take a married man for her lover. As she said the word to herself, it shafted through her heart and filled her with regret. She had

compromised her morals so much for this man. She
had allowed him such freedom with her body! Why
did his touch rouse such feelings, commit her to such
abandoned behaviour?

Pulling herself together, she tried to eliminate all
signs of his fervent attack.

For a while, she was unable to enter properly into the
fun of the party, her preoccupations with her own
emotions remaining paramount. However, the children
soon drew her into their joyous and uninhibited games
and she fooled around as much as the other three adults.

Saif was undoubtedly the children's favourite. He
was so strong that they were able to tumble and climb
over his body without fear of being rebuffed. Jeannie
watched him crawling over the sand on all fours,
almost bent to the ground from the weight of the
squealing children on his back, and her heart twisted.
What a marvellous father he must be!

Whatever game he played with the others, he always
returned to Stela and teased or played with her for a
while. The little girl's adoration was plain to see.

Ashti noticed Jeannie watching Saif's gentle
treatment of the child, and smiled. 'He is so good with
Stela. She loves him very much. And he loves her.'

'It's odd,' said Jeannie. 'I wouldn't have thought a
man like the Minister would be so compassionate.'

'No? Then, Miss Bennett, you don't know him very
well. And, of course, he knows all about handicapped
children.'

'What do you mean?' asked Jeannie.

'In his home . . .' began Ashti, only to rush over to a
child with a bleeding nose.

So that was it! One of his own children was
disabled. Poor man! She blushed at her behaviour.
Ahmed was right; she was behaving a bit like a tart.
And his poor wife! The woman not only had a

handicapped child to cope with, but an errant husband as well. She was far more to be pitied than Saif. Once again, Jeannie felt deeply ashamed of herself. For the sake of his wife and child, she must keep a tight check on her emotions. It was ridiculous to give in so easily to his touch.

Now the children were playing a version of blind-man's-buff. Everyone was mustered into a ring and one boy stood in the middle, wearing a thick blindfold. The ring danced around and stopped, each child and adult standing in silence. The boy felt his way to the ring, capturing a girl with his arms and feeling for evidence of her identity while everyone giggled as his hands teased her thick plaits. They were all shouting something at him now and, with a red face under the blindfold, he kissed the girl's cheek then stood back.

'Lele!' he cried triumphantly, and the children yelled their delight at his correct guess. Then Lele tied on the blindfold and the ring started its dance again.

Despite her inner pain, Jeannie couldn't help giggling. For a while, the pleasant warmth of the late afternoon, and the simple pleasure of the children, created an atmosphere of deep happiness around her.

Lele fumbled along the standing figures and they yelled at her to guess the identity of one of them, but she seemed to be searching for someone in particular. Her little hands stopped when she came to the Minister's Western trouser-legs. With a cry of delight, she pretended to examine his body and he bent down so she could rub his face and tweak his nose. Then she flung her arms around his neck and kissed him on his cheek. Swinging her on to his shoulders, he let her tie on his blindfold. For Jeannie, every action of his was a sweet pain, so much love did she feel for him at this moment.

He pantomimed silly actions as the children moved around him—staggering as though drunk then roaring like a lion when the dancing feet were stilled. Brushing imaginary whiskers, he knelt on all fours and stalked round the circle, lifting his head and roaring, sniffing the air as if following a scent.

To Jeannie's horror, he was making straight for her! She moved to one side, but the children pushed her back excitedly, their voices drowning Saif's as he stumbled nearer. Then his hands were on her ankles and she gasped to feel his warm hands curl around them.

He stopped, non-plussed, but the children yelled him on. He rose reluctantly and put out his hands, making a brief show of identifying her. To the urging of the children, he bent his head and gave her a token kiss on the cheek. Then he ripped off the blindfold, standing tensely before her, his arms hanging helplessly by his sides.

Ashti and Abdullah exchanged glances while the children tried to push Saif closer to Jeannie. He was oblivious to them, lost in Jeannie's eyes. With a sob, she tore herself away, running to her jeep which was parked outside the school. The children ran after her, thinking this was part of the game, but stopped when they saw her agonised face.

Saif spoke softly to the children who returned to the beach, Ashti and Abdullah hastily introducing them to another game even as their eyes strayed to the couple by the jeep.

'Jeannie!' came his deep tones.

She turned her back on him, tears welling up in her eyes.

'Wait there. I'll explain you're feeling ill and have to return. Don't go!' he cried. Not trusting her, he rapped out an order to his driver that Miss Bennett was not to leave without him.

To the wails and goodbyes of the children, he raced back to the jeep and instructed the driver to take it to

Safiq immediately. Taking a firm hold of Jeannie's arm, he walked her to his official car, the air-conditioned Mercedes, and pushed her inside.

He drove without speaking along the Safiq road and then turned off along a small track lined with frankincense bushes and oleander. Their heady perfume almost choked Jeannie.

The light changed to a deep rose-pink as the sky darkened. Night fell with characteristic abruptness, and Jeannie and Saif still sat in silence.

'You said we had some arrangements to make,' he prompted gently.

'Yes!' Her voice was vehement. 'You must leave me alone. I don't want to become involved with you. Said al Saif, I am attracted to you—it would be foolish of me to say I wasn't. But I'm not going to jeopardise my life by getting mixed up with you. So forget it. Find someone with fewer morals.'

'Morals!' His bitter laughter infuriated her. It was awful that he thought she was promiscuous, but she couldn't begin to deny it. 'You're no innocent. You forget, I left you unlocking one of the police flats with your own key. Besides, whenever I've held you in my arms, it would have taken only a few more moments before you were completely mine! If we had been in my bed, or somewhere more private, you would have given yourself to me!'

Her face flamed. 'I wouldn't have,' she retorted. He mustn't think that!

'Admit it, Miss Bennett, you're trying to capture me with your teasing. Give him a little, withdraw a little; it's an old trick, and it works very well on me as you can see.'

'I'm not doing anything of the kind!' she blazed.

'What an expert actress you are. Tell me how many men you have trapped.'

In a low voice, quivering with emotion, Jeannie plunged into deception. 'Oh, loads.'

'Sort of trapped,' she thought, keeping her fingers crossed behind her back.

'But it wouldn't do to become involved with you.'

'I can play the teasing game as well as you.' Saif pinned her arms behind her back and stroked her body with his free hand. His callousness outraged Jeannie and her responsive body infuriated her even more.

Abruptly she was released. With one long calculating look, Saif drove back on to the Safiq road. Jeannie clenched her hands into fists and balled them tightly in her lap, squeezing hard to release some of her pent-up emotions.

He was treating her like a plaything, but maybe she'd asked for it. It would need an all-out effort at the ball to put him off and ensure that the Minister never attempted to touch her again. His caresses were too dangerous, too deadly, for someone as inexperienced as she. If only he wasn't so persistent!

By the harbour wall, they both noticed a dishevelled Ahmed, his hair tumbled and uncombed, his shirt stained and unbuttoned. One of his shoes was in the gutter; he was holding the other.

With a muttered exclamation, Saif leapt out, then checked himself. Passers-by turned away tactfully. Jeannie stayed in the car but could hear every word.

'Ahmed, it's me. Let's go home. I have the car.'

Ahmed's sagging face lifted as he focused with difficulty. 'Siddown. Have a drink.'

'Later. We'll have one at home. Please Ahmed!'

'It's Kate, Kate, lovely Katie. Lis'n. Letter. Wantsh nu ... nuth'n to do ...' His voice trailed off and he drank deeply from the bottle he drew from his pocket.

Saif knelt in the dust. 'Come home. You look terrible.'

'I am. Sho unhappy, Shaif. Don't you be unhappy.'

'No, I won't.' With infinite tenderness, he helped Ahmed into the car and turned, stony-faced, to Jeannie. 'Please get out. You can walk to your flat. I'm going home.'

Miserably, she complied. Then, as her light salad supper lay uneaten in front of her, she tried to sort herself out.

No one could blame her for admiring Saif, could they? Everyone else did. He was a fantastic boss. Working so closely with him had resulted in her impression of him as a sensitive, compassionate man. She loved him, but the situation was hopeless.

Yet it seemed unfair that she should be the one to have to hold back; he was not prepared to deny himself any pleasures. Typical man! The ball would clinch things, she told herself. Either that, or she must go home.

She rang the airport, noting the times of the international flights, and also the infrequent hops from Safiq's tiny air strip to Abu Dhabi.

Within the hour, there was a ring at her doorbell. A sturdy figure clad from head to foot in a black *dishdasha* pushed straight past her. The woman wrenched away the concealing folds of her headdress to examine Jeannie intently.

'My name is Mahine,' she said.

Jeannie nodded. This was going to be very uncomfortable.

'You work with the Said?'

'That's right.' She imagined him with this woman who had borne his son. Mahine was at least twenty-five years older than he was. Once she must have been handsome; now her face was care-worn and furrowed, her small brown eyes furtive under greying brows.

'You not hurt him. Keep off. You give him pain. Go back to your land!'

'I am going, as soon as I legally can,' said Jeannie quietly. 'You mustn't think anything has happened between the Minister and me. It hasn't.'

'He kiss you!' she accused.

Jeannie hung her head. 'Yes,' she whispered. Was Mahine guessing? 'But it ended there. You must believe me. I've tried to avoid him ever since I discovered he was married to you.'

A gleam came into Mahine's eyes. 'Ah! Wife,' she said slyly.

'I found out ages ago, and I'm not interested in married men. It's not long before I leave Riyam. Please believe me.'

Her plea was so genuine, so agonised, that Mahine would have been very insensitive not to know she was telling the truth. 'Mees Bennett,' she said in a threatening voice, 'you see him, I make trouble. Yes?'

Jeannie nodded. It had made her feel worse, seeing Mahine, putting a face to the name. Poor woman, she must have a difficult job hanging on to Saif. And her child was a problem, too.

'I'm sorry, very sorry. Please forgive me,' said Jeannie contritely. 'I promise you needn't worry any more.'

Mahine left, obviously satisfied. Wordlessly, Jeannie shut the door behind her and shivered as she remembered the sight of Ahmed, a shambling drunk. If she didn't get out of Saif's life, he might turn to drink too. What an unfair world! Her life seemed to be one long continual denial of pleasure.

On the day of the ball, all official work in Safiq halted at lunch-time. That afternoon, Jeannie slept for a while, then gave herself over completely to an untypically selfish celebration of being a woman. Somehow she had to put the ghastly experiences of yesterday behind her, and work hard to achieve her aim.

So her skin was oiled, massaged and perfumed until she felt aware of every inch of her body. That was the trouble of course; acting in a sensual way tended to make her feel sensual. She must remember it was just an act.

Nevertheless, slipping on the moss-green dress made her feel slightly breathless and very decadent. It clung so smoothly that any underwear would show and she had never known the feel of shifting material on her naked body before. The dress was of fine silk, cut very simply with a figure-hugging bodice and narrow straps. The skirt fell full-length, slim and elegant, whispering over her hips. In the mirror she looked like a stranger; vibrant, glowing, an alluring woman.

Jeannie leant her head forwards and brushed her hair hard, catching it up into a knot on the top of her head and twisting it into a shining coil around which she fastened a spray of fresh jasmine. Despite her persistent smoothing, tendrils of hair escaped the knot and curled beguilingly around her ears and at the nape of her slim neck.

They irritated Jeannie. She wanted to look sophisticated. Whoever heard of a soignée woman with kiss-curls? Still tucking back her hair ineffectually, she opened the door to Ben's knock a little apprehensively. When he saw her, he stood as though stupefied.

'Am I all right?' she asked, concerned.

'Very grand,' he replied gruffly. 'We'd better go straight away.'

He was very quiet on the way. Since the Consulate was close by, they walked to the far end of the waterfront where it stood, brilliantly floodlit, at the extreme tip of the crescent-shaped bay.

Apart from the floodlights, the Italian-style façade was festooned with garlands of oleander and hibiscus, looped around the intricate carvings and ending amidst swathes of palm fronds on the crenellated roof. Soldiers, loaned from the Sultan's personal guard, and resplendent in red jackets and black sashes over gold trousers, flanked the wide marble steps. Drifting across the waterfront, came the sound of violins.

'The proverbial Arabian Night's dream!' thought Jeannie. And she was soon to leave it all. Her stomach churned. If only she didn't have to pay the consequences of an affair with Saif, she'd give in to him like a shot. Darn her conscience.

At the top of the steps, she stopped, surveying the golden lights of the grand hall and the sparkling ballroom beyond. The role she was having to play tonight of a heartless, narrow-minded racist filled her with nerves.

'Ben, you're very quiet,' she noticed finally. 'Have I overdone it?'

Under her hand, his arm twitched. 'No.'

'Are you sure? It's not too revealing, is it? I don't want to look cheap.' She became anxious.

'Fishing for compliments?' he asked roughly. 'Sorry,' he said quickly, 'you're a bit of a shock to the system. Never saw you quite like this before. You look fabulous. How on earth I'm going to work with you again I don't know. Make sure you save the first couple of dances for me. Then I can cool off.'

Silenced by his words, Jeannie allowed him to lead her inside. She'd never expected such a reaction. In a daze she stumbled over greetings to the British Consul and his wife, then several officials, all of whom had difficulty in wrenching their eyes from her. The women were critical, darting sharp glances. That was what came from not mixing with them, of course.

Sensing her nerves, and the thinly-veiled antagonism towards her, Ben claimed his first dance immediately. In her nervousness, Jeannie forgot the subtly daring dress which showed her body as surely as if she was naked.

Although she danced incessantly, giving the appearance of careless gaiety, all the time she was on tenterhooks, waiting for Saif. Maybe he was not coming. Her heart sinking, she excused herself from her most recent partner and slipped over to Ben at the bar.

'Drink?' he asked.

'Dry white wine, thanks.'

'You're the success of the evening,' he said proudly.

Jeannie smiled absently. 'My feet feel as flat as pancakes! I'm not used to so much dancing. Ben, didn't you say the Minister would be here?'

'Saif? I thought so. Maybe his wife made him stay home.'

Jeannie's face fell in disappointment. Seeing her dismay, Ben slammed down his glass in amazement. 'Good grief, Jeannie! Is all this dressing up to impress him?'

'Of course not,' she said defensively.

'You're not a very good liar,' said Ben. 'So, you're fascinated by him like all the others. Keep away, Jeannie! He's dynamite—far too experienced for you to tangle with. Even I can recognise his sensuality, and I don't fancy him! Let me tell you something. I had a very nice American nurse for a girl friend till he came along and stunned her with his good looks. He didn't *do* anything, just stood and had a drink with us. She shook like a leaf afterwards and I couldn't bear to ask her out again, I never had such an effect on her. She's over there; you'd better join her and form a queue for him.'

Jeannie was shocked and deeply jealous to hear of Saif's success. Across the room was a girl with short hair, glaring at her. Jeannie laughed. 'Ben! If that's your nurse, take another look. She's trying to kill *me* with her eyes. I think she's jealous.'

Ben followed her gaze. 'I think you're right!' he said slowly.

Jeannie pushed him off the stool and watched the girl accept his invitation to dance. She drained her glass and watched some important-looking people strolling down the red-carpeted staircase. To her disappointment, Saif was not among them. She studied the empty landing at the top for a moment, her heart beating quickly. The staircase was still empty.

And then, suddenly, there he was; standing arrogantly at the top of the stairs, surveying the crowd below. He looked relaxed and outstandingly handsome. His dinner jacket was expensively cut to reveal his magnificent body; his trousers perhaps a little too tight-fitting; the whiteness of his shirt echoed the whiteness of his teeth as he flashed lazy greetings to his friends below before wandering casually down.

As if drawn by a magnet, Jeannie moved towards him, then remembered her role. She flung her head back, smoothed her dress, and wandered slowly across his path, turning as if by accident. His response was more than gratifying.

Stopping in shock, his black eyes widened in disbelief, his gaze travelled in a detailed examination of her hair and eyes, lingered on her mouth, surveyed her slim neck and shoulders, and finally her breasts. Clenching and unclenching his fists, he raked his gaze over her hips and then stared insolently at the outline of her legs under the thin silk.

His visual assault had shaken her to the core. Gathering all her wits, she moved nearer, smiling coolly.

'Good evening, Said al Saif,' she said huskily.

'Miss Bennett.' He seemed unable to say more.

'Would you like your eyes back now?' she asked daringly.

'Sweet Allah!' he muttered under his breath. 'You

have more than my eyes, Miss Bennett.' He stepped close and took her in his arms. She gasped in protest but he danced her on to the floor, his steps smooth, his body insistent. A slow waltz. Drat his luck!

'I didn't hear you ask me to dance,' she cried, trying to quell the rising excitement. Her body was answering his presence and the gently sensual beat of the music.

'Perhaps not,' he growled. 'I'm trying to avoid a scandal. If I hadn't taken you into my arms then, my response to you would have caused considerable embarrassment to everyone. And since it was you who caused my arousal, it seems fair that you should cover it.'

At his words, Jeannie flushed deeply, lowering her head in acute shame and seeing to her dismay that even the bare half-moons of her breasts were pinkening. She felt very naked, very aware of his hand sliding around her waist and drawing her closer. Her breasts pressed against his jacket and she could feel his excitement, his hard maleness pressing into her loins, demanding and receiving a response from her.

Shivers ran down her back. He must feel the burning of her hips—it felt to her as if they were on fire. Miserably, she tried to pull away, and he leaned back to look at her. She averted her gaze.

'The dress suits you,' he said in flat tones. 'And under that hard exterior is a soft woman waiting to be discovered.'

'Well, don't think you're going to do the discovering,' she said sharply.

'But your body smells of the perfumes of Arabia. Aren't you planning a seduction?' he whispered.

'Naturally. But not for you.'

He stopped suddenly and several couples collided with them. 'Who then? I demand to know.' He held her wrist tightly.

'Please! People are looking!' She wrestled surreptitiously with him as his hand gripped her delicate bones.

'I must know. Outside! We'll discuss this.'

'I'm not going anywhere with you,' she retorted, frightened.

'You want to discuss it here then?' he grated, standing his ground.

Jeannie drew in her breath. Curious eyes turned towards them and tongues began to wag. In desperation, she agreed. Her plans were going wrong. Saif's powerful masculinity made her dizzy, unable to think straight.

CHAPTER SEVEN

'IF you think you're taking me up there, you're mistaken,' she said, indicating the broad steps which spiralled in front of them.

'They lead to the roof, not bedrooms,' mocked Saif. 'We won't be alone. There'll be others, cooling off.' His eyes slanted wickedly at her.

'There'd better be. And let's hope you cool off while you're up there.'

The roof was vast, edged with terracotta pots overflowing with yellow mimosa. Saif drew her to a seat with a panoramic view of the harbour. It was very romantic. Moonlight silvered the water, breaking into splinters of light as the waves rolled in lazily from the Gulf. Small fishing boats trimmed with lights waited for the sardine to run, their nets spread from boat to boat in a visible circle.

'Safiq!' breathed Saif. 'How I love it.' He faced Jeannie. 'And you—you'd ruin it all!'

'Me? I don't understand.'

'Oh, if only I knew... Are you really after some poor devil here, or are you still playing games with me? Whatever your reason for wearing that dress, you're playing with fire by tempting me.'

'I didn't intend . . .'

'Maybe. Maybe not. But you're not indifferent to me.'

Jeannie struggled for composure. 'Your imagination is way off target,' she said. 'Just wishful thinking, I suppose,' she added with enforced flippancy.

'You bitch!' he spat. 'It must give you a great deal

of amusement to have all those men panting around you like the dogs in Safiq *sukh*. What do you allow each one? A few kisses, a touch here and there . . .'

Jeannie cracked her hand across his face in blind fury. He made no attempt to stop her but gave a bitter, twisted smile.

'Obviously the truth. Nasty, isn't it? And I'm caught in your web, too. Trouble is, Miss Bennett, I'm not like your compatriots. You've made a mistake, pushing me so far. By Allah! You're ravishing!' he breathed. 'Quite irresistible. Let me tell you this: I don't put out my own fires. I expect the person who lights them to do that. Come here!'

He pulled her further into the corner, where they were completely concealed by parlour palms. As his intentions became obvious, she shook her head, a sick feeling in her stomach. Brutally, he gripped her chin in his strong fingers and tipped it back to kiss her. From under her lashes, two hot tears dropped, burning her fiery cheeks.

To her surprise, the expected violent assault never took place. Gentle fingers brushed the tears away and as she opened her brimming eyes, he groaned softly.

'God, how I hate myself,' he whispered. 'I want to hurt you. I have to. But all that happens is that I get more hurt than you do. You don't understand yourself, that's the trouble. Until you do, I have no chance at all. One day, maybe. I'm not sure I can be that patient.'

'I don't mean to hurt you,' she said through her tears. 'Why can't you leave me alone?'

'If only I could. Dear Allah, if only I could!'

His lips tasted the salt tears. A shudder rocked through her body and he ran his hands around her small waist. Placing her hands against his chest, she shook her head again to deny him, mistakenly raising her eyes to look deep into his. Their expression of sadness and caring rendered her helpless.

With a muttered oath, he leaned forwards and pressed his lips full and hard against her mouth so that she could feel the pressure of his teeth for a brief moment. Then he was twisting, tearing at her lips with his, flickering his moist tongue between them. His hands ran down the bare flesh of her back and her body obeyed his call. She strained towards him, trying to quench the violent emotions she felt, sweetly moaning as he worked passionately on her mouth till she could hardly bear it, wanting him to stop, wanting him to continue for ever.

'Open your mouth, sweet flower,' he murmured. 'Open it!'

Nervously, she parted her lips and his tongue darted inside, hot, probing, wakening within her a groaning demanding fire which thrust sharply through her body from her breasts to her thighs. She gripped his shoulders and pulled him closer, her tongue answering his, fighting to touch his lips, his mouth.

For a moment he released her, his eyes clouded in passion. She felt his trembling hands slip the straps from her shoulders. Delicately, his fingers ran over her skin till every muscle, every nerve, willed him to explore further. A hand caressed the silk over her breast and slid into the dress, quickly finding the erect nipple under the slippery material. In sudden shock, she started at the wild sensations he was creating within her and her own hands reached for his chest, running over his hard muscles, slipping inside his collar.

Somehow, unbidden almost, she found her hands unbuttoning his shirt till she could slide her hands over his smooth, warm and throbbing flesh, trailing her fingers over the dark glossy hairs of his chest. He groaned, kissing her almost cruelly, running his hands down her sensitised body. Then, suddenly, he rose with an angry oath and hastily rebuttoned his shirt. Only then, waking to reality, did she hear someone calling his name.

His hands shook uncontrollably. He was beside himself with passion.

'Minister al Saif! Anyone seen him? Minister!'

It was the Consul's aide. Saif pushed his way through the palm fronds.

'There you are, sir. Sorry to bother you, but you're needed urgently at home.'

'Hell! Tell them I'll be back later,' Saif interrupted curtly.

'I'm afraid it's important.'

'It always is. Later, I said. Leave me!' he ordered.

He was returning to Jeannie. She looked up and saw the aide close behind him, twisting his hands anxiously.

'Sir . . .'

'Not now!' yelled Saif.

The aide refused the suggestion. 'It's your brother, sir.'

Saif froze. 'Ahmed? Now what? Tell me, man!'

Catching Jeannie's eye, the aide chewed his lip awkwardly.

'Damn you, Jardine!' cried Saif. 'What's happened?'

'Bad news, sir.'

Saif sank to the seat beside Jeannie. 'Go on.'

'Perhaps you'd prefer privacy, sir?'

'Tell me!'

The aide fiddled with the buttons on his jacket. 'We've just had a call from the police. I'm afraid your brother was found in the sea by a fisherman. Just over there.' He pointed to the rocks at the base of Fort Jehan. 'Witnesses saw him on the tower earlier. He must have thrown himself off—maybe a couple of hours ago.'

'Ridiculous. Of course he didn't throw himself off. He must have fallen. Is he badly hurt?' asked Saif.

'I'm afraid there was a note, sir. The police are treating it as suicide.'

Shock quivered through Saif's powerful body and there was a long silence. 'Suicide! Ahmed is dead?'

'I'm sorry, Minister. I haven't explained very well. Yes. He'd hit the rocks and was washed into the sea.'

'He could have been attacked—robbed—someone might have . . .'

'Sir, there's no mistake. The note was quite explicit; he said he was going to take his own life.'

'Ahmed, may you be in God's keeping.' Saif ran his fingers through his hair. 'Perhaps if I'd paid more attention to his problems rather than my own . . .'

'Will you go home, sir? The Chief of Police is making enquiries there.'

'To hell with his enquiries! I can save him the trouble. He was murdered—driven insane with grief. Curse that woman! Curse every woman from that damn country!' grated Saif. 'May they rot in hell!' He rose to his feet, swaying and clutching at his stomach. He looked ashen. 'I feel sick,' he whispered.

'You'd better get home. Can you drive, miss? I'd take him but I think he needs a friend at a time like this.'

'I'm the last . . .'

'Here, quickly, or you'll have a problem. The Minister seems to be in a state of shock. Get him home as fast as you can.'

The aide ushered them down a back staircase and into a small courtyard where Saif's own Aston Martin was parked. In a waking nightmare, Jeannie slid into the driver's seat, nervously testing the accelerator and listening to the engine's throaty growl.

'Turn right, then to the market and up the mountain road. You can't miss the house—it's the large white one,' said the aide. 'Thanks a lot. Hurry now.'

Jeannie drove like an automaton, unwilling to face up to what had happened, not daring to look at Saif who sat hunched by her side. On the mountainside, she stopped at a pair of massive ornamental gates. He looked up wearily and pressed a switch in the car. The gates opened to reveal a long drive flanked by lush vegetation. In the darkness ahead loomed a large and imposing white building, set to catch the breezes from the west. A beautiful and magnificent house. His home. And his wife's.

She drew up and the sound of the engine died away, leaving an awful dead silence in its place. For a moment, Saif sat still, unable to move, his teeth clenched tightly, fingers digging into his palms. Jeannie felt desperately sorry for him. Tentatively, she stretched out her hand, all her instincts yearning to comfort him.

'Don't touch me!' he yelled. A look of agony passed over his face and his voice shook with emotion as he continued: 'If I'd been thinking less of you, preparing for the ball, hoping you'd be there ... May Allah forgive me for putting you before my own brother. Go and play with some other man's heart, Miss Bennett. Mine's empty.'

He lurched out of the car and Mahine ran from the house to help him. With an angry, vicious glance at Jeannie, she disappeared inside, tenderly supporting Saif.

Jeannie waited, sick with misery, unsure what to do with the car. In a few moments, Mahine reappeared.

'Go,' she said, her face distorted with hatred. 'Take the car. He says go. Out!'

In anguish, Jeannie drove back to the flat, careering wildly down the narrow mountain road. She raced up the stairs to fling herself down on her bed, bursting into a torrent of tears at her own grief and his.

For some hours she cried, till her face was red and puffy from weeping. Then, her body dead and drained at last, she rose to drag off the ballgown and to shower in icy water, the sharp needles of cold shocking her into awareness. Briskly she rubbed herself dry and pulled on a cotton nightdress.

She'd made a mess of everything. Oh, she'd discouraged him with words, but they'd both known she hadn't meant them. And she'd ruined a lot of people's lives in consequence. Every bone in her body, every ounce of common sense told her how wrong she was to be attracted by Saif, let alone allow him to touch her. You had to walk away from committed men, she knew that. People's emotions were too fragile to be played with.

There was only one thing to do. She must clear up any outstanding work and leave as soon as she could get a flight.

Why hadn't she met him before he married that bad-tempered middle-aged woman? If Jeannie had been his wife, he wouldn't have had that chip on his shoulder about English women. Ahmed might even be alive. On the other hand, perhaps Mahine wasn't bad-tempered until she discovered Saif was a philanderer. Which came first, Jeannie wondered, his infidelity or her harshness? He was such a ladies' man. The gossips spoke of little else. She tried to imagine how she would feel, married to an unfaithful husband—even if he was Saif.

From his reaction, it was obvious that he'd never trust her again; that was something she must get used to. Jeannie had come a long way since her arrival in

Riyam. Now she knew why men and women behaved in a seemingly irrational way; how complex they were. Facing the truth about herself, she realised that all her reserve in the past had ill-prepared her for the flood of emotions that Saif had aroused.

It was a very chastened Jeannie who resumed work. Whoever took over from her would find everything in perfect order, and her task was made easier by Saif's absence. Jeannie was dreading their next meeting and started nervously when Ben put his head around the door of his office.

'Oh, it's you,' she said in relief.

'Right first time. Just to remind you that I'm going to Sheddah tomorrow.'

'O.K., Ben,' she said. 'I think your nurse is going to miss you.' She felt jealous of his happiness.

Ben's eyes crinkled. 'Mmm. Actually, we're sort of engaged,' he said shyly.

'Oh! I'm so pleased.' She walked over and kissed his cheek in delight. Her pleasure was cut short by an angry snort from the doorway.

'Leave my male staff alone, Miss Bennett. Seduction after office hours, if you please,' growled Saif.

She whirled round. He was blocking the doorway with his massive bulk, dark and saturnine in his fury.

'Oh, no,' began Ben.

'I don't want explanations. I'm too busy and I'm not a fool. Here are the papers for Sheddah.' He thrust them out at arm's length and Ben took them, highly embarrassed.

'Ben, I'd like to talk to Miss Bennett in private,' said Saif.

Throwing a warning look at Jeannie, Ben walked out, reluctant to leave her to explain.

'I'm sorry,' began Jeannie.

'For flirting in the time I'm paying for?'

'I—oh! You take my breath away with your prejudices! I wasn't flirting. All I'm interested in is doing my job.'

'That's debatable. Still, your probationary period is nearly up. Soon you'll be gone. What do you care?'

The slow colour slid up Jeannie's face. How did he know that she'd decided to leave Riyam? She'd given no indication.

'As I thought,' said Saif. 'Your face betrays you. Why bother to stay here until then? Go now. Let someone else take your job—a man who will take a serious interest in my country, not use the opportunity to find a lover or to fill in time between assignations.'

'I have a contract to complete,' she said in a furious voice. 'I'm doing the best I can, Minister.' She almost ground out the words, giving his title a derogatory sound. 'You can't deny that what I've done is good.'

'Some.'

She tilted her head so she could look at him, hating to feel him despising her so.

'Damn you, I'm as good as Ben.'

'Tell me,' he grated, 'will you miss Mr Chatsworth when you leave?'

'Of course.'

'As I thought. Now allow me to come to the reason I came to see you. Not thinking, of course, I'd break in on a sultry session.' He stifled her gasp of anger with a brief wave of the hand. 'As I said, I'm busy. I don't want to go over the matter again. I came to say that there's someone I want you to fit in as a pupil teacher in one of the schools in Safiq. She's honest and eager to learn.'

The Minister shouted a name over his shoulder and a girl entered the room. Jeannie's eyes narrowed; it was the girl from the oasis—the girl he had fought for.

Ye Gods, so he'd been keeping her somewhere all this time!

'I refuse to employ her,' she said firmly.

'I ask only as a courtesy. I could insist.'

'Insist all you like.'

'I want a reason for your refusal.'

'It's not my policy to employ cast-offs from your bed. If I did, we'd soon be overstaffed.'

'What!' he yelled. He turned to the girl and spoke sharply to her. She left. Saif strode furiously up to Jeannie, his face black with anger and pushed her back till she was trapped against Ben's desk. Jeannie beat her fists helplessly against his heaving chest, terrified at the consuming darkness in his face.

'Stop pushing me around!'

'You deserve to be beaten,' snapped Saif. 'I can't believe how you formed such an extraordinary impression of me. I don't know what gossip you listen to, but it's wrong. That girl has never been in my bed. She's been studying English all this time.'

'You fought for her!' accused Jeannie.

Saif let out an exasperated sigh. 'You really imagined I was claiming some kind of rights over that child? I wouldn't be so foolish—and I'm certainly not that desperate. Listen, the man I restrained was the girl's uncle. In accordance with Riyam tribal laws, he was about to kill her. She'd dared to look longingly at me. And, before you jump to conclusions, I didn't encourage her. I didn't even know she was following me around the village.

'You must know it's considered a dishonour for a young girl to pursue a man; a dishonour punishable by death. I had to stop her uncle. He was wild with fury and misery. So I held him by brute force till he agreed to release her into my protection. By doing that, no one, including me, could touch her. Just one more thing. If you were to employ all the women I've made love to, you'd be understaffed. I'm fussy.'

Jeannie hung her head. His story rang true. 'I apologise. Forgive me,' she said.

'Yes, I always will.' The sadness in his voice touched her.

Without realising it, she arched her back towards him. Her breasts strained against the thin material of her dress. At that moment, Ben walked back in.

Saif turned on his heel and pushed past blindly.

'Jeannie.' Ben came close.

'It's not what you think,' she said miserably.

'Don't kid yourself,' he said. 'Jeannie! I warned you. You're attractive, and so is the Minister. It was bound to happen. You're very naïve, Jeannie, and you just don't understand what an impact you have. He's too much for you. He has a grudge that he'll never overcome. I told you not to tangle with him, so take my advice. I feel responsible for you. He's bad news, Jeannie. Let him have you and he'll use you and chuck you away.'

'Why do you say that?' she asked, her eyes shining with tears.

'Everything points to it. Do you know that his father deliberately starved himself to death?'

'No!' cried Jeannie, horrified.

'It all came out yesterday at the enquiry into Ahmed's death: the family history was dragged through the courts when Saif had to give the background to the suicide. It can't have been easy for him, going over the tragedy again. When Saif's mother deserted them, his father went into a decline, refusing food, refusing to care for the boys.'

Jeannie remained silent. No wonder Saif was so angry and so distressed. He couldn't have been much more than nine years old when he was left, motherless and fatherless, to roam the streets with his brother.

'Poor Ahmed really buckled when his marriage collapsed. You can see how a liaison with another Englishwoman would tear the family's emotions apart.'

'Then why doesn't he leave me alone?' muttered Jeannie.

Ben shrugged. 'As I said, you're very attractive. It could be that the English blood in the Saif brothers makes them susceptible. But I think there's even more to it than that. I reckon he's going to use you to avenge his father's death—and now his brother.'

'What do you mean?' Jeannie clasped her hands to her chest.

'You forget, for all his education Saif is very much a Bedouin and revenge is a powerful and important part of his nature and his code. I'm afraid he might try to break you to redeem the honour of the family.'

'I think you might be right,' said Jeannie, trembling at her narrow escape. 'He told me about vengeful tribesmen once, but I never thought to apply it to him. He seemed above all that. I once imagined he . . . Oh, Ben! I'll never forgive him for leading me on so!'

'Try to understand it from his point of view. He's racked with pain. He's had a hell of a miserable life.'

Jeannie took a deep breath. 'I think I have to accept that his hatred is real and his charm is all a pretence. Now I'm definitely leaving, Ben. I couldn't possibly stay.'

With the realisation that she had been set up came initial pain and then a rueful self-deprecation. She had been a fool to tangle with a man like Saif and to imagine that he cared for her.

There were just two days to go now before she took

her plane home. Memories and thoughts fought to crowd her mind as if to intensify her last hours in Riyam. Routine work turned out to be the best antidote, and she was therefore engrossed in checking receipts when she became aware of a woman standing hesitantly in the doorway of her office.

'Excuse me.' The woman slipped off her tan-coloured hat, exposing neatly waved silver hair. 'I was sent by the receptionist. Apparently I have to see you, but I really need to see Said al Saif.'

Jeannie extended her hand in greeting. 'That's right, I'm Jeannie Bennett. Do you have an appointment?' She was searching Saif's diary which had been transferred to her desk. He had been absent from the office for a while now.

'No, no appointment. There wasn't time to arrange one—I came on the first plane I could.'

Strange how agitated the woman was. The lines of her once attractive face were tense, as though she faced an unpleasant task. Jeannie felt sorry for her. There was an air of sadness underlying the anxiety.

'I'm afraid the Minister isn't available. There's been a family tragedy and he rarely sees anyone now. I can't say when he'll be back. Can I help at all?'

The woman sank into a chair, slumping wearily. 'Oh, Lord.' She looked up and smiled wanly. 'Forgive me. It's just that I've been steeling myself to meet him for the whole journey. It seems almost an anti-climax not to beard him in his den. How well do you know him?'

'Quite well,' murmured Jeannie, mystified.

'My name is Mary Denyon. I'm Lynette's sister.'

Apparently the names should have meant something to Jeannie, but they didn't. She tried to look attentive.

'This is difficult for me,' said Mary. 'I'm so relieved that I don't have to face him, but it does create problems. Look, I have some items that must be returned to him personally. Can you arrange that?'

'Not really. I'd like to help, but . . .'

'Perhaps he'll change his mind when he hears my news. It'll cheer him up, I'm sure. Perhaps you could get a message through to him saying that his wife has just died.'

Jeannie was stunned. 'What did you say?'

'Oh, yes. I'm the bearer of glad tidings,' said Mary dully. 'Tell him she died a week ago.'

'You must have the wrong man,' cried Jeannie. 'His wife is alive. She's here, in Riyam!'

'Here? The bastard! So he took a second wife after all! He was married first to my sister, Lynette.'

Horror spread through Jeannie like a sickening wave. If this woman was speaking the truth . . . she'd been worrying about upsetting one wife when he was actually married to two!

'My sister came to live with me when the Said rejected her. A few years ago she developed cancer.'

'This is awful. I'm so sorry,' murmured Jeannie, thinking hard. She made a rapid decision. Saif must know. This poor woman must complete her business with him and get herself back to England; she was obviously too distressed to be here.

'I'll drive you to his house. We'll camp out there if necessary until he sees you.'

'Thank God! I didn't want to come all this way for nothing. They told me at the Riyami Embassy in London that it would be unwise to send valuables by post.'

In order to get the experience over quickly, Jeannie took Mary up to the house immediately. The huge iron gates were shut and no one answered the bell there. Slowly, she drove around the high perimeter wall, hoping to find another entrance. There was, a small ornate side-gate. The two women stood by the wall listening the faint sound of a child's voice. Thick tangles of jasmine hung over part of the gate, their delicate perfume floating on the gentle breeze. Jeannie pushed the fronds aside impatiently, lifted the latch and walked with Mary into the exotic garden.

This was his home. Here in this paradise of orange trees and limes, cool ferns and glorious flowering shrubs, sweetly singing birds and fragile butterflies, he played with his child. In the glistening white house, rising to her right, he spent his nights with Mahine. Thank heavens she had not allowed herself to become involved in his complex sex life. He was incorrigible.

Jeannie tried to control the shaking of her legs. At least she could put him squarely in the wrong now. That would give her satisfaction. Yet she bit her lip in distress. Her idol was turning out to have more clay on his feet than she ever imagined.

The sound of laughter was louder. Breaking through thick shrubs, they saw a boy aged about eight, rather clumsily throwing a ball for a small dog to retrieve. Sometimes his aim took the ball rather close to the oval swimming pool that glared its brilliant blue back at the sky.

On the edge of the huge expanse of lawn that stretched from the house terrace sat Saif, slumped in a chair against a marble pillar and pouring whisky into a tumbler. He looked awful, grey-faced and hollow-eyed.

There was something odd about the boy's speech as he yelled at the dog. Saif raised his head and grumbled in Arabic about the noise. His son ignored him, tussling with the dog. Jeannie was about to step on to the lawn when the boy jerked convulsively and thrashed around, screaming and making a terrible choking sound in his throat.

'Malik!' Saif flashed across the lawn and held his son close, trying to draw him away from the pool and receiving vicious blows to his face as he did so.

'Mahine!' he yelled.

With all his strength he struggled to contain the boy. Jeannie couldn't bear to hear the child's thin strangled screams or to watch the terrible scene as Saif clung desperately to his son, a look of intense misery distorting his face. The screams died away and Jeannie risked a glance. Now the boy lay tucked on his side, at peace, while Saif gently stroked the sweat-streaked hair from the child's forehead.

Mahine was wringing out a cloth that she had dipped in the pool. She knelt to bathe the boy's face, then helped him to his feet and into the house.

Saif returned dispiritedly to his chair. It was a bad moment, Jeannie knew, but she must make a move sometime. Beckoning to Mary, she stepped on to the lawn. The whisky bottle slipped from Saif's nerveless fingers, smashing at his feet.

'You!' he groaned. 'In the name of God, I have enough torment without your adding to it.'

'I wouldn't have disturbed you,' said Jeannie stiffly. 'But I had to bring your sister-in-law. She has some news.'

'My what?' He rose from the chair unsteadily.

Mary Denyon was shaking her head. 'Miss Bennett, this isn't Saif. He's too young.'

'Who the hell are you?' yelled Saif.

'Mary, Lynette's sister.'

His face registered shock and he gripped the chair for support. 'You can get the hell out of here. You're too late if you're after money. My father is dead. Your sister has no claim on the estate now—the inheritance has passed to me. I am Tarik al Saif.'

'So you're Lynette's son. No wonder she idolised you. And yet you're as cold a bastard as your father. Relax, I haven't come for your wretched money. I want nothing from you—quite the contrary, in fact.'

'So why are you here?' growled Saif.

'Does it interest you to know that your mother has just died?'

'No.'

'Exactly the reaction I expected! To be so unmoved by your mother's death ... Here.' Mary thrust a box at Saif. 'These are Lynette's rings and her jewellery from your father. I believe they're very valuable. You can do what you like with them, I don't want them. And these are your father's unopened letters that I intercepted to save Lynette grief.'

'Grief! My mother never felt grief. She was a hardhearted bitch.'

'How on earth would you know?' replied Mary with spirit. 'You'd never say that if you'd seen her face when she had your father's first letter. It broke her. Why didn't he have the decency to discuss a divorce face to face, instead of waiting till she was visiting me?'

'My father wouldn't behave like that.'

'Oh no? Read his letter for yourself; it's in that damn box! Every time Lynette weakened, I made her read it to remind her what a bastard Saif was.'

Angrily, Saif turned the key and unlocked the box. A much-read letter lay on the top. He scanned it, his face darkening in even greater fury.

'It's typed! It could be from anyone. In any case, he couldn't have written anything like this—he was too tender-hearted.'

'Tender?' scoffed Mary.

'Yes, tender! Everyone here knows he killed himself in grief. He'd hardly send his wife away and then

proceed to starve himself to death. Surely you can see
that doesn't make sense?'

'That can't be true!'

'Ask anyone here. It's common knowledge.' Saif
shook his head emphatically. 'Your sister has played
on your emotions. It was she who refused to return to
us. I know my father died for love. I lived through
every terrible hour of it. Yet that's his signature!'

He motioned them to sit down and his voice grew
ominously quiet. 'I have an idea. Mahine was there
when father received the letter from Lynette, asking
for a divorce. She knows everything that happened.
Mahine!'

Jeannie wrinkled her brow. Saif's wife a contemporary of his father? It was possible, but it didn't
make sense.

Saif handed Mahine the crumpled piece of paper.
After reading the first few words, her hand flew to her
mouth and she stared at Saif in horror.

'Well?' he growled.

'*Inshallah!*'

'Dear God!' he breathed. 'It was you!'

Mahine wrung her hands and nodded.

'You wrote it? You typed that letter?' he asked.

'Yes. Me.'

His strong arm shot out and gripped her wrist,
pulling her close. 'Why? Why in the name of God did
you ruin our lives?'

She shrugged. 'I love.'

With a face like thunder, Saif released her as though
he couldn't bear to touch her. 'Get out of my sight!' he
whispered.

He sat down, deathly still, shutting his eyes. His
face seemed to crumple. All the life in him seemed
drained away and he spoke quietly to himself,
forgetting Jeannie and Mary.

'I always knew she wanted him. I never knew how devious she was. Ironic, the havoc one woman can create.'

'What will happen to Mahine?' asked Jeannie tentatively. In his present mood, he might harm her.

He sighed. 'Nothing. I can't even throw her out. She's under my protection.'

'I don't understand,' began Mary.

He raised a heavy head. 'I need her,' he said simply.

Jeannie longed to comfort him, to throw her arms around him and say how much she loved him, that she would stay after all. But his words stopped her in time. He needed Mahine, even though he had made the painful discovery that she really loved his father. That was what happened between couples; they grew used to each other. The bonds were strong. Jeannie thrust her hands through her hair. Suddenly she had to get away. She could not stand being here. Taking advantage of Mary's sympathetic overtures to Saif, who sat with bowed head, Jeannie slipped back into the shrubbery.

In her haste to escape, though, she had turned in the wrong direction. She found herself in a small private garden, thick with heady perfumes. Lemon trees bordered the stone walls and roses intermingled with thick frankincense bushes. Thorny myrrh trees formed an avenue along a central path, their trunks slashed to exude their oily resin. Jeannie inhaled the powerful incense. It filled her with evocative memories. A soft sigh fell from her lips, a sigh of despair.

Gentle hands held her shoulders and her immediate reaction was to lean back in quiet acceptance for she knew whose they were.

'Jeannie, why leave now?' Saif's voice was charged with emotion. 'Don't run away. I need time to think, time to re-adjust. All my life I've thought . . . Well, I want to forget that. Thank you for bringing Mary here. I've asked her to stay so that we can heal old wounds. And I need to learn about my mother; all I have is fragments—the scent of frankincense on her clothes, English tea on the lawn . . .' Saif was struggling with the bitter-sweet memories.

'I'm pleased,' Jeannie said evenly, steeling herself. 'I'll leave, then.'

'Don't go,' he said huskily.

'I really must. I've lots to do,' she said brightly.

'Hell, woman! I mean don't leave Riyam! There's no reason to go.'

'Of course there is. I'm packed and my replacement is flying out in two days.'

'I'm not asking you to stay in your job. I'm asking you to stay here with me.'

How could he ask her! A quick replacement for his wife, she supposed. Poor Mahine, settling for the son when she had really wanted the father. It must have hurt Saif's pride to know he was second best choice.

Saif was holding her in an insistent grip. 'Have you any idea how I feel about you? How you fill my life, my thoughts? It's time you listened to your inner feelings, Jeannie. Imagine waking up beside me; imagine living in this house, walking in this garden. That would be living!'

His words and the passion in his voice staggered her. Dumbly she stood, refusing to look at him at all. With a muttered exclamation he slipped his arms around her as if she was a fragile butterfly.

'No! Oh no.' Her lips parted in unconscious seduction, craving the pressure of his mouth.

'You're irresistible! Even if you say no, you mean yes, you know that.' He bent his head and ran his fingers sensuously across her cheekbones and mouth, then massaged the nape of her neck. Deep thrills travelled through Jeannie's body. His warm lips pressed the hollow of her neck then his teeth nipped lightly at her flesh in barely controlled passion. He crushed their bodies together, raising his lips to her cheek, tantalising her by first denying her a taste of his mouth, kissing the path of her cheekbone in slow deliberation.

'I can teach you so much about yourself; inch by inch, mouthful by mouthful.'

She moaned and twisted her mouth to his, arching strongly against him and tugging on his black curls so that his head bent fiercely to deepen each kiss. 'Just once more. Just this once. A last embrace before I leave!' Her head resounded with the plea to her conscience.

Wildly, she raked his hair with her hands, the shafts of excitement running through her body in shocking bursts of heat. Lowering his head, that beautiful, strong and lion-like head, he brushed his lips over the madly beating pulse in her throat; his quivering hands moving to the curve of her hips. As she grazed the corner of his carved mouth with her fingers, he caught them in his strong teeth, gently savaging them with restrained passion. Her body melted into his, her fevered mind knowing only the desire welling up in her submissive flesh. She loved him.

The sweet Arabic words he murmured, husky and throaty, drove him insane with overwhelming emotions. His powerful muscular legs forced her hard against the wall, and a pleasurable trembling sped through her when he shifted his body. He wanted her. He was highly aroused and she was not sure whether she could refuse him.

'You mustn't go any further!' she attempted.

'There's nothing to stop us. I no longer feel

revenge, just love. Dear Allah, I love you, sweet Jeannie.'

At last he had said the words she longed to hear and they almost broke her weakening resolve. She shut her eyes, listening as he declared his love, memorising every phrase and the inflection in his voice to store as a memory in her loneliness in England.

Her silence had been taken for acquiescence. Saif began to explore the small buttons down the back of her dress and she started at the touch of his burning hand on her back.

'Don't fight it. I love you, remember? Admit that you love me and don't be afraid.'

Her small trembling hands fluttered helplessly against his chest. He whispered tenderly, a low sound deep in his throat, frightening her with his intensity. He gathered her more tightly in his arms and slipped one hand downwards to cover the rising swell of her breast, groaning softly as her warm body rose to his touch.

He seared his lips over her eyes, her lips, behind her ears and down the line of her jaw, setting up an exquisite agony in her heart. It was such a practised seduction, she told herself.

'No,' she moaned but he silenced her with his lips, murmuring her name in a low rough voice which almost broke in its urgency.

'Sweet flower, don't deny me. I'll never hurt you, trust me.' The weight of his body trapped her, his iron hard thighs filling her with weakness at the male strength within them. Her body grew limp and he took the opportunity to whisk her into his arms, striding purposefully through the garden, into the house and up a broad staircase.

Enclosed in his powerful arms, her senses in a riot, she spoke urgently to him, afraid to cry out in case Mahine heard and should surprise them. He only held her tighter and strode on. Then they were in a room: a bedroom. He kicked the door shut with his foot, tumbled her on to a huge bed and eased himself on top of her.

Jeannie was in despair. His idea of love was not hers. He knew no bounds of decency. If he loved her, he wouldn't treat her like this.

'Please don't do this to me; it's humiliating!' she begged.

'Trust me, I said,' he answered as if to a child.

'When will you realise that it shames me to be thrown on to your bed like this as if I was a prostitute! Where does your Bedouin sense of honour come in?'

Puzzled, he stroked her cheek. 'There's no shame. Let yourself go, you hold back too much.'

'I've let myself go more than I should. Please let me get up.'

'Not until you admit what you feel for me. I'll do anything in my power to make you own up to your feelings.'

He rippled delicate fingers across the risen peaks of her breasts. Traitorously they swelled even more under his touch. Again he reached around to loosen more buttons.

'I'll yell!' she threatened, hoping this would stop him.

'Nobody will hear. The walls are thick. Anyway, no one would dream of coming into my bedroom.'

All the time his fingers had been moving rhythmically, insisting on a response from her body. Her head began to toss from side to side in abandon and with a groan her mouth sought his. She raised her body to lie against his as it arched over her and allowed him to rouse her tongue with darting assaults. The soft yielding of her body encouraged him to slip down the top of her dress, then to slide his hands over her slim hips till he ground his whole weight down on to her.

'Kiss me, kiss me,' he muttered, closing his passion-filled eyes.

With fast-beating heart, she slipped her hands to circle the pillar of his neck, devouring his mouth, answering kiss for kiss, demanding to be loved by him. His lips ran a firm moist path over her shoulders, her arms, and then he slid the clothes from her body, moving down to caress her now naked breasts and to take each nipple in turn into his hungry mouth. She pushed her hands wildly through his hair, crying aloud her need for him. Yet this time, he gave a deep shudder and pulled himself away, staring at her flushed and delirious face.

'Now tell me that you love me,' he said quietly. 'Tell me.'

He watched, a burning challenge in his eyes. Once again, his fingers drifted over her hips. A deep juddering jolted her body; she felt as though she had been set alight. Every nerve was jangling for him, for her to be his, till she cried involuntarily: 'I want you. I love you. Oh dear heaven, I love you!'

The blazing light in his eyes softened. Gently, he stroked her forehead, brushing back the golden hair which flowed on to the pillow. Jeannie held her breath, torn by her overwhelming love as he wrung from her every drop of moral strength she possessed. She put up her hands to his chest in denial.

'No? Really no?' he sighed. 'All right. I have what I wanted. My sweet girl, do you know I would have driven us both mad with excitement to hear those words?' He looked down on her, lying so innocent in her seductiveness on his bed. 'I adore you. I want you . . .'

His words were broken short as his bedroom door was flung open. Mahine stood glaring at them. Saif rolled over abruptly in shock. Jeannie drew in her breath noisily, covering her bare breasts with her hands.

'How dare you enter my room!' yelled Saif.

Mahine stayed silent, tight-lipped.

'OUT! Shut the door!' Saif flashed an anxious glance at Jeannie but her eyes were shut in deep embarrassment. She had to get out. In one swift movement, she raced for the door, struggling to pull her arms into her dress and pushing past the startled Mahine. Hurtling down the stairs, with Saif's cries echoing after her, she stumbled into the garden. Only then did she notice that she was barefoot.

The scene in the bedroom was impaled upon her memory; Saif on the rumpled bed, his chiselled features and tumbling curls, his horror at Mahine catching them together . . .

Panting heavily now, Jeannie ran through the confusion of trees and plants until she came to the little gate. Small stones cut her feet but she ran on unheeding, tearing open the door of the jeep with shaking hands, pressing hard on the accelerator and concentrating all her thoughts on the road as she swung too fast around the hairpin bends of the track and screeched finally through the city gate.

No one had followed her. She felt no disappointment in that. The whole episode had to be erased from her mind. She'd been so close to becoming his mistress— ye gods, how stupid she'd been! He was too persuasive for anyone's good. No wonder he made so many conquests.

At her flat, she grabbed her bag and thrust in a few personal possessions. Dragging on another pair of shoes, she caught a glimpse of the twin bottles of frankincense and myrrh. She removed their stoppers, sniffing the fragrances as though to record them for ever. Then she flung the bottles at the wall with a final angry yell.

CHAPTER EIGHT

SHE arrived at the airport to find one standby seat on a
flight leaving in ten minutes. Formalities were waived
as she sprinted over the tarmac accompanied by a
porter, her hair flying wildly behind her. She
staggered weakly up the steps and collapsed, emotionally and physically exhausted. The engines
whined, roared, then thrust the plane forwards along
the runway. Safe at last!

Leaning back, she searched miserably for glimpses
of the country she had come to love. As the plane
taxied down the runway, a green Aston Martin sped
under the airport lights. It swerved straight into the
perimeter fence and Jeannie held her breath at the
impact. Saif leapt out, waving frantically. The plane
banked and her last view was of him clinging to the
mesh fence like a trapped animal.

They were now over the bay of Safiq. Little boats
bobbed gently on a navy-blue sea and the white
crescent of houses receded into the distance. Never
before had she felt so utterly defeated by life. This was
an accumulation of failures; her father, her mother,
and now the man she would have made her lover—
these she had loved and these she had lost. This was
the last time she'd give her love to anyone. What pain
it caused! If only she had relied on her head and not
her heart. Once again, Jeannie Bennett had to return
to her remote self.

She could not remember the flight; she had no
memory of eating, speaking to anyone, arriving at
Heathrow or hiring a car back to the flat. Thank

goodness her cousin had left. She could not have faced
sympathy from anyone.

How cold, grey and unfriendly England seemed.
Her flat felt the same. Most of her plants had died and
were limply accusing her. She threw them out and
tried to warm herself up. It was mid-December and
dreary after the warmth of Riyam. For half an hour
she sat close to the gas fire, sipping sweet black coffee
spiced with cinnamon in the Arab fashion.

She couldn't stay here, she'd only brood. And she
didn't want any contact with people she knew; they'd
ask questions about Riyam and she couldn't bear to
discuss it.

Scanning the educational advertisements, she found
a teaching post which also offered accommodation.

At first, it was a little nerve-racking since she had
never worked in a girls' boarding school before. She
slept badly and lost weight, not caring about her
appearance. In sensible skirts and flat shoes, she
looked the archetypal spinster. Which was what she
was, of course.

The Minister would approve, she thought, then
chided herself for the memory.

He would come unbidden to her mind when she was
reading poetry to the girls, or explaining a piece of
literature which expounded on love. All she could do
to shut out that time in Riyam merely brought the
events more sharply into focus when thoughts of him
intruded. It would take some time to heal the wound.

One sunny winter's day, she was sitting on the
school steps in discussion with her English group. Liz,
one of the girls, was having difficulty in understanding
the problems posed in the book they were reading.

'I can't see why they don't defy convention,' she
protested.

'Because when you do so, you also invite pain,' murmured Jeannie.

'Better than leading a boring life,' said Liz, unable to refrain from looking pointedly at Jeannie's drab clothes. 'Now, what I fancy is a Heathcliff! Why can't we do *Wuthering Heights*? Lots of lovely passion!'

'Hmm, maybe. But what a lot of agony it brought,' replied Jeannie.

'And excitement, and undying love,' cried Liz. 'Wouldn't you rather have that, and lose it, than not have it at all?' She sneaked a look at Jeannie who was staring into space.

'Miss Bennett!' The headmistress broke in on the conversation. 'A prospective parent is arriving. Very insistent on an appointment, he was, and his English was quite appallingly limited. You know some Arabic so I'd be grateful if you'd show him around. He'll be here soon. I had to use pidgin English to make myself understood. Let's hope his daughter is a bit more coherent!'

After her initial shock at hearing that she would have to speak a language that she would rather forget, Jeannie smiled her agreement. 'Yes, of course I will. How old is the girl?'

'No idea, I couldn't understand him when I asked. We'll have to make an assessment when she arrives. I'd like to take this girl, Miss Bennett, the family is very influential. Do your best.'

The girls were full of curiosity and stayed to see the visitor. They all had romantic notions of Arabs, dreaming that one would whisk them away to an oasis paradise. Jeannie knew otherwise. Most Arabs married so young that they'd had a wife in the background since teenage days.

She sat on the grey stone steps, half-dreaming. When a large black car with CD plates drew up, she realised too late that she had not been given the man's name. How embarrassing! She watched a small man slip quietly from the passenger seat. The girls were whispering. She turned, irritated at their bad manners, and when they pantomimed admiration she frowned warningly at them.

'Heathcliff!' breathed Liz.

Jeannie glared at their scorn for the little man, then in a split second she realised that they really were starry-eyed. She whirled around, knowing before she saw him who the driver was. Her knuckles scraped against the wall as she steadied herself.

Saif's liquid eyes glowed. He stood fiercer and harder than before, more merciless, the civilised elegance of his charcoal grey suit contrasting with the raw passion in his face, his tightly clenched hands and tight jaw.

The small man glided up to Jeannie and bowed. 'May I introduce the Said al Saif, madam?'

Jeannie pulled herself together. Luckily, the girls were too overcome by Saif's masculinity to notice her shocked response. 'How do you do?' she murmured politely, longing to check her hair and to tuck in her baggy jumper.

'How do you do?' he returned, his strong tanned hand holding hers longer than custom allowed.

'I have been asked to show you around. I understand you speak little English,' she said sarcastically.

His eyes mocked her. 'Thank you.'

The girls followed them as Jeannie showed Saif the hall, the dining-room and the library, then made her way to a classroom. He had made no comment so far and Jeannie had filled the silence with nervous chatter.

'This is where the first-years work,' she said. 'How old is your daughter?' More revelations—a daughter of school age! How much more was there to know about this man? Angry jealousy flooded through her.

'No age.'

'What do you mean?'

'She hasn't been born yet.'

'Then you're wasting our time,' snapped Jeannie sharply. How dare he put her through all this, standing so close and looking at her in that way!

'I think you are wasting my time!' To her astonishment, Saif took both her wrists in a vice-like grip. Behind them, the girls gasped with delighted shock.

'If you don't let me go, I'll create such a fuss that there'll be hellfire raging between us,' she threatened in a low tone.

'Try it.'

'Release me!' she whispered furiously. 'I don't care how you got here, but . . .'

'It was British Air,' he interrupted, grinning. 'I would have flown on the wings of a butterfly if I thought it might do any good. Do you remember that butterfly at the oasis?'

Him and his seductive voice—of course she remembered the butterfly! 'I meant, how did you find me?'

'By searching the records of every educational establishment in Britain. A long job, as you can imagine.'

'And what do you want? I presume it's not to weigh up the possibilities of this school?'

'Correct. I want you.'

If only he'd keep his voice down! The conversation was becoming embarrassing. 'I'm not available.'

'Dear Allah! You're married?'

'No!' His distress had shaken her. He still cared.

'I'm not surprised,' he laughed, 'in those clothes.'

'Will you leave or do I send for the headmistress?' seethed Jeannie, absurdly angry that he found her unappealing.

'I will leave after we have had a talk. Come with me somewhere—a tea room, a café, I don't care—I must talk to you.' When she remained silent, he shook her gently. 'Jeannie, I've flown thousands of miles to speak to you. Allow me that, at least. I'll stay, and compromise you dreadfully if you don't,' he added wickedly.

'Damn you, Saif. All right, I have a free period coming up. You've destroyed my English lesson for now. Liz, please tell the Head that I'm showing Said al Saif the town. I'll be back for prep duty.'

'Oh, yes, Miss Bennett,' said Liz breathlessly.

Jeannie knew she would never live down his appearance at the school, nor the familiar way he was treating her. She allowed the little Arab to tuck her into the back seat with Saif who sat carefully apart from her, his arms folded, staring at the scenery with interest.

At the café, the waitress gazed soulfully at him, writing down his order automatically while concentrating on his high-boned face and sensual mouth. He smiled kindly at her and she dropped her notepad.

Stupid woman! How silly to fall for his studied charm. Yet Jeannie's own legs quivered and she wrapped them around the table leg in front of her. The tray of tea was reverently placed before Saif and a pile of cakes temptingly slipped by his plate. Even the ladies sipping tea and nibbling Danish pastries were entranced by him. Yet his eyes were only for Jeannie. He reached over and loosened her hair from its untidy knot at the back of her head.

'Corny, I know, but I hate your hair tied back. It's too beautiful to hide,' he said.

'You once ordered me to do it that way,' she reminded him.

'Ah, yes. But I had to stop your attractions distracting me. You've lost weight.'

Darn her baggy clothes! 'So have you. Now tell me what you want to say. I don't have much time.'

'I want to ask why you left.'

'Why . . .! What else did you expect!' Jeannie lowered her voice, aware that everyone in the room was straining to hear their words. 'You take me to your bedroom, try to seduce me, then in walks Mahine . . .'

'Yes, Mahine. That startled me, too. She's never invaded my privacy before. But she's not important.'

'I can't believe it!'

'It must have embarrassed you. Let's start again. Come back to me, come back *with* me.'

'If you've come all that way just to say the same things, then you've wasted your time,' said Jeannie tightly. He hadn't changed a bit; he was totally amoral.

'And we both lead a life without love? For the first time in my life, I can reach out and be happy. The same goes for you too. You know we're right for each other. Why fight the situation?'

'I couldn't give myself to you, knowing about Mahine and the child,' said Jeannie, hating the idea of going over the same ground again. It was too painful.

'Oh.' His voice grew sad and disappointed. 'You know about Malik.'

'I certainly do. I don't break up families. Part of you would always be committed to them.'

'Not much of me.' He sighed deeply, his eyes yearning, pleading. 'As a matter of fact, Mahine has moved out with Malik. There wouldn't be any awkwardness now they've gone. I came here hoping that you'd missed me enough to want me now. Would you come back with me, Jeannie?'

She shook her head in frustration. Would he never understand? She leaned forwards, speaking slowly and clearly. 'Saif, I don't believe in living like that. While you have a wife, you're just not eligible.'

'A what?'

'Mahine, damn you!'

A slow smile slid over his face. 'Mahine?' Sweet Allah! Now I understand. You little fool!'

He shook his head in amusement. Then, throwing back his head, he roared with laughter, rocking back in his chair, startling the tea-room with the deep resonant sound.

Embarrassed, Jeannie put her hands over her face; he prised them gently apart.

'Jeannie, listen to me. Mahine's not my wife, she merely looks after Malik. I never married—there was no woman I wanted. Till I met you.' He grinned wickedly at her. 'Mahine was put under my father's protection when she was a child—just like the girl at Fallah. You remember when you thought I was fighting for the girl?'

Jeannie flushed scarlet. Another stupid mistake? Her heart was lifting.

'Mahine grew up idolising my father and wanting to marry him. But he fell in love with Lynette. It was because of Mahine's jealousy that she was packed off to London, to train as a nurse. She was damn good at that.'

'Your father took her back.'

'As a nurse, my nurse. Immediately Mahine qualified, my mother persuaded father to send for her. She looked after Ahmed and me till father died, when she disappeared—she'd returned to her family to grieve in private, giving no thought to us at all. Much later, I sent for her to help with Malik. Ahmed's son was a difficult child, excessively irritable and suffering from fits. Kate wouldn't look after him: she wasn't interested. So it was natural that we should ask

Mahine to care for him. We owed her a living, after all, and we didn't want strangers to know that Kate was behaving so badly. A matter of pride.'

'Wait a minute,' breathed Jeannie. 'Did you say *Ahmed's* child?'

'Well, who else's? Mine? I wasn't married, was I?'

'But I thought . . .'

'Ah, now I understand your modesty. And why you thought I was so callous. Poor Jeannie! Can you see why I needed Mahine? It was hell at home with Malik, Kate and Ahmed, all so aggressive and bitter. I felt very bad-tempered at times.'

'You were bad-tempered!'

Grinning, he caught her hand, leaning closer, not heeding the stares from everyone in the tea-room. 'So, no more troubles. I've had enough. You know, I was furious when Mahine walked in. I was just about to ask you an important question and she ruined the moment. I'm afraid I was pretty foul to her.'

'So she left.'

'She felt guilty every time she looked at me, knowing what she did to mess up things for my family. Malik is in London, by the way, for treatment. Apparently he has some inborn deficiency. And the treatment is simple, I gather, just a case of some vitamin additive to his diet. He'll be monitored for a while, then we can fly home with him.'

'We?'

'Did I say we? How odd.'

'Oh.' Jeannie tried not to let the disappointment show in her voice. 'I'm glad about Malik, poor kid. You said you were going to ask me something.'

'Did I?' he asked innocently.

'Maybe,' thought Jeannie, 'I'm hoping too much. Maybe he wasn't going to suggest . . .' Her teeth caught her lower lip as it trembled, and a wave of misery flooded through her. 'It is these awful clothes and no make-up! He's seen me for the frump I am. If only I'd known he was coming!'

'Look at me,' whispered Saif.

She shook her head, unable to speak.

'You'll have to do as you're told when we're married,' he said. 'I expect total obedience.' His tone was teasing. 'Did you hear what I said, Jeannie?'

Saif began to kiss her fingers and Jeannie was very much aware of the frisson of shocked excitement which ran around the café, the entranced waitress, and the fact that her lips had stopped quivering. She raised brimming eyes to his face.

'Married?' she said in a husky voice.

'Of course. You don't think I'm wasting the air fare for anything less, do you?'

'Blast your economy measures!' laughed Jeannie.

'Sorry. I thought something like that would appeal to your careful nature.'

'I'm not sure I have a careful nature. I don't really know myself as well as I thought.'

'Then we'll discover you together. You trust me?' asked Saif.

'I trust you.' And she did. That such a powerful and charismatic man should love her was breathtaking enough. That he should be as gentle and tender as she had always dreamed was a miracle. 'I trust you totally.'

'My flower opens at last. Time I gathered you up before anyone else is drawn to your sweet nectar.'

'Don't make fun of me. I know I look awful.'

'You need a mirror. You're radiant. A bride already. Well—' he paused as a look of intense desire crossed his face '—almost. Tomorrow morning I'm getting up at dawn to plead with every official who can arrange instant marriages.' He searched her eyes and saw an answering passion there. 'Perhaps not at dawn. Perhaps . . . Just where do you live, Jeannie?'

'In the school,' she breathed.

Saif smiled. 'I think we've shocked them enough for today. Shall we go to my hotel, instead?'

'Oh! I'm supposed to be on duty later.' She broke off, confused, as he took her face tenderly between his hands.

'I'm damned if I'm letting you go now I've found you. Don't worry, I'll ring from the hotel. I expect those girls have spread a few rumours by now— enough to keep your staff room going for years.'

Jeannie laughed at the idea. They left the tea-room, and the warmth of his body enfolded her as they walked the few hundred yards to his hotel. Other lovers strolled along the Georgian-fronted High Street, engrossed, entwined in each other. Saif bent to kiss the top of her shining head.

'For years I've envied couples like this,' he confided. 'Now they envy me.'

Gently his strong arms pulled her closer, snuggling her against his chest, enfolding her till they were in his room.

He pushed the door shut and Jeannie leaned back on the hard wood, closing her eyes. All she could hear was the gentle rise and fall of his breath.

'Jeannie, I don't think you'll ever know what this moment means to me,' he whispered. 'At last I can stop fighting my need for you. I can give you everything, without reservation.'

'Draw the curtains, please Saif,' she murmured.

'If you like.'

She heard the swish of material, then soft music filled the air. Almost immediately his lips were caressing her face, the poignant scent of frankincense wafting from his shirt.

For a moment he broke away, slipping off his jacket and tie. Tenderly he caught her by the waist and lifted her bodily on to the bed reaching down to unfasten her stockings and teasing her bare toes with his tongue before flicking tiny kisses to the top of her legs. Gazing into her eyes, he unzipped the drab skirt and slowly, sensuously, removed her jumper. Jeannie reached up to him, running her hands over his biceps and chest, fumbling impatiently with the buttons on his linen shirt. She pressed her lips to the dark silken hairs on his chest, savouring the warm scented maleness of him.

He seemed so experienced. She might disappoint him. She couldn't compete with the sophisticated women he must have known.

'I don't know what to do,' she said uncertainly.

'I do. Leave it to me. And you *will* know what to do. Give in to your instincts, Jeannie; respond to your feelings.'

Lowering her to the pillow, he removed the rest of their clothes with a few swift, expert movements and she lay nervously quivering under his impassioned gaze, tremulously avoiding his nakedness by keeping her eyes shut.

'Sweet Allah! You're so beautiful! Don't be afraid. We have all the time we need.'

His kisses rained down on her till she writhed with pleasure among the smooth sheets, answering his restrained fire with flames of intensity.

Curving her back, she pressed hard against his smooth body, burning her flesh into his. At last she felt his full weight come down upon her. His ragged breathing pounded in her ear as he chewed gently at her lobe, then slowly, inexorably, his lips stole to her mouth, taking it roughly in his possession.

She had for so long refused to believe that any

lasting pleasure could be gained from surrender. But in the desperate pleading of his eyes and the love in his face, she finally surrendered her heart, her mind, her soul: the feeling of total release raising in her an uncontrollable passion that could no longer be denied.

'Saif,' she said softly. 'I love you.'

He tried to speak, and failed. Instead, he kissed her deeply, the wetness of his cheeks merging with hers.

'My first love,' he murmured at last. 'My only love.'

With infinite tenderness he unleashed at last all the deepest emotion that had been trapped in her. She gave herself utterly, withholding nothing, till they both slept exhausted, curled inseparably, united now in those private shared moments of passion and trust. Jeannie had found the man she loved.

Coming Next Month

2815 DRAGON SEA Bethany Campbell
Dragon Sea, the deserted stone mansion she loves, should have been hers. So how can this young Maine woman accept the new owner—the very man who destroyed her dreams once already?

2816 WALK INTO TOMORROW Rosemary Carter
A teahouse proprietor in the Canadian Rockies needs to get over the trauma of the past before thinking about the future. But the persistently friendly owner of a local hotel won't wait!

2817 PLAIN JANE Rosemary Hammond
Seattle's most eligible male hires a garden editor to landscape his new home, and then pursues her. Irresistible men don't pursue plain-Janes with any serious intentions, do they?

2818 THE GLASS MADONNA Liza Manning
The respected master of dei Santi Glassworks expects an older, more mature student to train with his traditional craftsmen—someone who's come to Italy to learn about Venetian glass, not love. What he gets is Miranda....

2819 WILD FOR TO HOLD Annabel Murray
Hard times force a determined tomboy and her grandmother to sell their Lake District farm. But when the new owner tries to control more than the land, he has a fight on his hands.

2820 INNOCENT IN EDEN Margaret Way
An assistant scriptwriter discovers scandal in an Australian family's past...and a fiery, consuming love that's very much in the present.

Available in February wherever paperback books are sold, or through Harlequin Reader Service.

In the U.S.
P.O. Box 1397
Buffalo, N.Y.
14240-1397

In Canada
P.O. Box 603
Fort Erie, Ontario
L2A 5X3

Six exciting series
for you every month...
from Harlequin

Harlequin Romance·
The series that started it all

Tender, captivating and heartwarming...
love stories that sweep you off to faraway places
and delight you with the magic of love.

◆

Harlequin Presents·
Powerful contemporary love
stories...as individual as the
women who read them

The No. 1 romance series...
exciting love stories for you, the woman of today...
a rare blend of passion and dramatic realism.

◆

Harlequin Superromance®
It's more than romance...
it's Harlequin Superromance

A sophisticated, contemporary romance-fiction
series, providing you with a longer,
more involving read...a richer mix of complex plots,
realism and adventure.

HARLEQUIN HISTORICAL

Explore love with Harlequin in the Middle Ages, the Renaissance, in the Regency, the Victorian and other eras.

Relive within these books the endless ages of romance, set against authentic historical backgrounds. Two new historical love stories published each month.

HIST-B-1